COAL TOWN STORIES

COAL TOWN STORIES

Cultural Cohesiveness Transcends
Generational Poverty

**AS TOLD BY MO HEALY
LEON SWARTS, AUTHOR**

PALMETTO
PUBLISHING
Charleston, SC
www.PalmettoPublishing.com

© 2024 Leon Swarts

All rights reserved.

No portion of this book may be reproduced, stored in a retrieval system, or transmitted in any form by any means–electronic, mechanical, photocopy, recording, or other–except for brief quotations in printed reviews, without prior permission of the author.

Paperback ISBN: 979-8-82295-812-8

TABLE OF CONTENTS

Acknowledgment vii
Jello xi
Prologue xv
Chapter 1 - Introduction 1
Chapter 2 - The Stories Begin 5
Chapter 3 - Home for the Holidays 11
Chapter 4 - Great-Granny's Story (Part I) 15
Chapter 5 - Bobbie Joe's Story 45
Chapter 6 - Great-Granny's Story (Part II) 52
Chapter 7 - Granny's Story 71
Chapter 8 - Sally Mae's Story 101
Chapter 9 - Presidents and Poverty Stories 114
Chapter 10 - Mom's Story 118
Chapter 11 - Mo's Story 145
Chapter 12 - Willie's Story 159
Chapter 13 - Town Stories 181
Chapter 14 - Other Towns 199
Chapter 15 - My Story 203
Conclusion 210
Epilogue 217
Afterword 219

ACKNOWLEDGMENT

I sat alone in front of the woodburning stove in an old country store and watched the sparks float off the logs and quickly disappear. I thought about my life and the changes and adaptations I made through the years. A descendant of Italian ancestry, I was born in Buffalo, New York, raised as a Catholic, and lived in a Northern culture most of my life.

My first exposure to Southern culture took place when I attended a small college in Western Kentucky. After graduating, I met my wife, went back to my hometown, and worked as an English teacher. During the next thirty years, I visited Kentucky a number of times. I didn't have a choice because my wife was a Kentuckian.

During the holiday visits, I met a lot of people who were born and raised in Louisville and rural communities across the state. I traveled throughout Kentucky for years and learned about its big-city and small-town cultures.

After retiring, we moved to Kentucky and bought a farm in Shelbyville, a small rural town between Louisville and Lexington. It's been a farming and dairy town since its settlement in the late 1700s. Families have worked the fields to grow tobacco, soybeans, hay, and corn for generations. The agrarian lifestyle has produced a strong family work ethic and community bond.

Since moving to Kentucky, I've met a lot of old-timers who have a story or two to tell. While sitting in front of the stove, one of those old-timers pulled up a chair and sat down beside me. We sat without saying a word to each other for the longest time. I had seen Barry in the store several times, and he never said much to me. He'd been farming since he was a boy and had a weather-beaten face to prove it.

We stared at the opening in the stove and watched the red-hot embers that glowed brightly under the logs. Unexpectedly, Barry asked me if I liked Jello. I looked at him, not because the question was odd, but because he hadn't uttered a word the whole time we sat there till now. I knew his question was intended for me because no one else was sitting with us.

Barry spoke with a country accent that I had become accustomed to during my six years of traveling across the state. Although I had been exposed to many Kentucky dialects, I still had difficulty understanding some of his words. His dialect was definitely Eastern Kentucky and obviously Appalachian.

I accepted the question that he directed toward me and said, "My mother made Jello for our family all the time when we were kids. It was a special treat after our Sunday afternoon dinner."

Barry looked at me with his steely gray eyes and said, "I got a story about Jello. Would you like to hear it?"

It was a frigid winter day, and I planned to sit for a while until the wind and snow died down. "Is the story about you?" I asked.

"I'm not sure who told the story to me. Maybe it was Mama. I don't remember. You know, sometimes stories are told over and over again, and the stories that's said a second or third time are never the same. So, maybe the Jello story has changed after being told so many times that it's different from the first time. I'm going to tell you the story the way I remember it and use the accent the way it was told to me," he said.

The story was told firsthand in the early 1930s with a country dialect. When I decided to use the story in this book, I wasn't sure I would remember all of its pieces and the dialect in which it was told, but I thought it would add to the storytelling approach I was using.

I'm going to share that story with you and try to include the dialect as I remember it. If it's not correct or you are offended, I apologize. It's just a story!

JELLO

What you eatin'?

Jello.

I ain't never seen nuttin' like that before. Where'd ja get it?

My mama made it fer me.

How'd you git it to be green and wiggle like that?

My Mama made it so it would taste like a lime and shake like yer shiverin'.

I'm going to tell my mama about it and see if she could make me some. Mama, this boy at school had this green stuff called Jello and it wiggled all over the place when you touched it. Can you make some?

Mama looked away and said nuttin'.

Days later, Daddy came through the door shakin' his hands together and just as happy as could be. Mama axed what he was so excited about. Daddy said we are gonna have a big frost tonight, and I'm gonna catch me a mink down by the creek. Daddy always said catchin' mink was better when it was winter. We could sure use the five dollar it'll bring.

That nite we all went to bed early because we knowed Daddy would be gettin' up before the sun. I laid awake for a while before fallin' asleep thinkin' about why Mama didn't answer me when I axed her to make me some green Jello. That's all I had on my mind was that boy's Jello.

When I got up Mama told me she was gonna make Jello today. She told me to open the box on the kitchen table and pour it inta a bowl. When I looked at what was in the bowl, I told Mama the Jello was no good because it wasn't green and didn't wiggle. I kept complaining, and before long she told me to put my snow boots on. She didn't tell me to put my socks on.

When I came back to the kitchin table, she was pourin' hot water in the bowl and mixin' the green stuff with a spoon. When she finished, she told me to put my coat, hat, and mittens on and take the bowl outside and sit next to the well and let it set there till it gets hard. I set there for a long time wit the cat tucked inside my coat to keep warm and wait for that Jello to get hard. Before long, the water turned green and hard, and when I touched it, it was shiverin' as much as me. When I got back to the house, I began eatin' the Jello and still shakin' like crazy from the cold.

About that time, Daddy came through the door and tossed three mink on the floor next to the potbelly stove. He told me to gut them and put them in a cloth sack. He knew that the mink would bring fifteen dollar. He took one look at me shiverin' like a scared cattail. He whispered somepin' in Mama's ear and walked out the door. He hopped in his '39 Ford truck and speeded down the road. I axed Mama where Daddy went and when he was comin' back. I thought sure he was mad at me and Mama, but I didn't know why. I thought maybe the Jello had something to do with it. Mama said she didn't know where he was goin' or when he was comin' back.

After a while, I saw Daddy's truck come up the drive, and in the back of his truck was a big box. He came through the door and set the box on the floor. He took a heavy white thing out of the box. I axed what it was. He said it's called an icebox, and now you can have Jello anytime you want.

I went to sleep happy that Daddy came home, Mama had an icebox, and I would have green Jello forever.

Barry finished the story. I was pleased that I understood it and, more importantly, the message it delivered.

My story acknowledges the storytellers of all time. Without their spoken and written words, there would be no record of cultural changes and differences that have contributed immeasurably to American history.

PROLOGUE

Storytelling, written or spoken, is a way to preserve history. I have no idea when the first story was told. I'm not sure that historians could tell you either. Stories are a record of the past, words for today, and information for the future. Of course, firsthand stories are more authentic because they come from the originator. Stories that are told second or third-hand often lose details, which results in a loss of credibility.

Have you ever played the party game *Tell a Story*? A short story is told to one person and then others. By the time it goes around a group, the story is not the same. This also happens when interviewing. If the story is firsthand, authenticity increases. The accuracy of a story told over time provides consistency. If a number of storytellers relate similar or identical information, it reinforces the story, and it becomes more credible and authentic.

I believe there are good and bad stories, whether spoken or written. The key to good storytelling is to make the story imaginative, humorous, suspenseful, interesting, and unique.

Coal Town Stories is a collection of stories about the settlement of a Scottish family in a coal-mining town in Kentucky. The stories are first, second, and third-hand, told by family members, friends, and townspeople. Their stories provide a cultural legacy that will be told for many years. Without their stories, we wouldn't know the past, present, or future of the fictional Coulton, Kentucky.

While drafting the story, I thought about using an approach that would take into consideration all the proper guidelines for proficient spelling, accurate punctuation, appropriate grammar, and a wide vocabulary. However, given the circumstances, the story wouldn't then be real. When we have a conversation with relatives or friends, we don't stop and think about what and how to say something—we just say it. I believe in most cases; we just express ourselves comfortably and honestly.

My intention is to do just that. The interviewing process used to tell the town's stories reveals the personal feelings and beliefs of families, townspeople, and the larger community. For this story, I believe that an interviewee's words and sentences should be written literally. If a sentence runs on, a word is misused, grammar is incorrect, or the dialect is questionable, the story will have more credibility.

Not using the best English might be heresy to publishers, authors, English teachers, and university professors. I agree that authoring a book requires formality, and the best English language characteristics should be used. However, when writing a story authentically, it should be written the way it is told.

Most book editors consider fundamental standard English requirements. Within the corrections category, spelling and grammar are important. Accurate spelling is essential because a misspelled word might be misconstrued as another word and would jeopardize the meaning and point of view of the story. Appropriate grammar is relevant when serious academic, historical, or nonfiction books are authored. Within the *refinement* category, clarity, conciseness, formality, punctuation, and vocabulary become writing characteristics that become essential to the genre of book or story that is being written.

Because the interviews conducted in this story are informal and spontaneous, exact punctuation, grammar, syntax, and spelling are not essential to comprehension. More importantly, the way in which the interviewees express themselves adds to the credibility of their stories. An informal style allows the reader to feel the words and incidents told. Without this approach, a story could be interpreted differently and not reflect the author's point of view.

During the interviewing process, the interviewees didn't stop in the middle of a sentence to consider their grammar, vocabulary, or conciseness. They spoke from their mind and heart without considering formality. If an interviewee thought about all the appropriate language requirements before speaking, how good would their story be?

Why do most authors have their books or stories edited? One, they don't want to be considered illiterate. Another possibility is the story requires corrections and refinements. Some books, however, are best written informally so the reader can step into and feel a character's feelings and emotions.

Whether you agree or disagree with this story's writing style, my goal is to offer a sensitive, enlightening, entertaining, and unique reading experience. Each book or story requires its own personal style. For me,

Coal Town Stories was best written and is best read with a less formal and more authentic approach.

Please consider turning to the first page and beginning.

CHAPTER 1
INTRODUCTION

Poverty is widespread among all geographic areas of America. It exists in small and big cities from east to west and north to south. The universal belief that poverty is confined to large cities is a misconception. Poverty is widespread in villages and towns regardless of size and population.

This story takes place in a small, fictitious town in Eastern Kentucky. Coulton is located in Harlan County and borders West Virginia and Tennessee. It is approximately one hundred miles from Lexington. Its population fluctuates from day to day depending on births, deaths, and families and individuals coming and going.

From year to year, Coulton's population is approximately six hundred. Most of the families have spent their entire lives in the town and have experienced poverty from generation to generation. A cultural bond of more than two hundred years is the glue that holds them together.

The main character in the story, Mo, was born in Coulton and is the youngest member of the fourth-generation Healy family. Her grandmother and mother were born in the same house near Swallow Hollow on the eastern side of the Appalachian Mountains.

The story traces the history of Mo's family from 1925 to 2024. It begins with her great-grandmother's (Peg) arrival in America when she was fifteen years old with her great-grandfather (William), who was twenty-five. The generational story offers a cultural description of her family's journey and subsequent settlement in Kentucky and describes the struggles and challenges families in a small mining town encounter.

Mo describes how her great-grandparents quickly found out that the cultural norms they were accustomed to in Scotland were dissimilar to those in their new home. Customs, traditions, language, and social interactions were distinctly different in the Appalachian region where they settled.

The Coulton culture was rooted in the early 1820 settlement of the Irish and Scottish, who left the British Isles because of territorial disputes and physical confrontations. The early Appalachian settlers possessed old-world characteristics and an isolated, clannish, tribal structure. The warrior culture created a continual battle over land and resources. The Scottish cultural characteristics were acquired from generations of regional wars. The Scottish region that William and Peg came from was rural but devoid of a warlike mentality. Their newfound culture in Coulton was different, and they were forced to adapt to survive. They were able to assimilate and make changes that were handed down through four Healy generations.

The plot encompasses an Appalachian coal-mining region in Kentucky where poor families have developed a strong bond spanning more than two hundred years. Mo (Maureen Healy McGuire), an investigative newspaper reporter, interviews her granny, mother, friends, and townspeople and writes about the embedded culture that still exists today. The story concludes with Mo's personal accounting of her life growing up in Coulton.

Mo works as a journalist for a Lexington newspaper that's struggling to survive. The editor knows that Mo grew up in poverty in a small Kentucky coal-mining town and asks her to tell her family's story. Mo accepts the challenge and uses a direct interviewing process with family, friends, and townspeople.

She begins the interviews with her granny. Granny describes her mother's (Mo's great-grandmother) 1925 journey from Scotland to Kentucky and her life in Coulton. She also recounts the stories her mama told her from ages six to fifteen.

Mo's first interview with Granny describes her mother's early life in Scotland, her marriage, her reasons for emigrating to America, and both the good and troubled times encountered in a new country. She details the cultural adaptations her mother had to make to survive. Mo gets a surprise when Granny gives her a box filled with her mama's diaries. Granny tells a firsthand story about her mama and daddy in their interviews and describes situations and events related to her mother's growing-up years, struggles she encountered, and positive memories of her past and present life.

After Mo's interview with Granny about her great-grandmother's story, she conducts additional interviews with her mother, brother, friends, and people in the town, some of whom are descendants of the original Scottish settlers. Their stories reveal their feelings about living in a small mining town in Eastern Kentucky, trying to preserve their Scottish culture, and adapting to a new one.

Mo concludes the interviews with a description of how the individual stories affected her personally. Despite the struggles and challenges the Healy family encountered over generations of poverty, her family, friends, and fellow townspeople survived and developed the strong cultural bond that exists today.

CHAPTER 2
THE STORIES BEGIN

THE STORIES UNFOLD WHEN THE chief editor of the *Gazette* requests that Mo travel to her hometown, Coulton, to write a story about her family, their struggles with generational poverty, and the effect it all had on developing a strong cultural bond among people in the town.

Mo has been a reporter for the *Lexington Gazette* for two years. The newspaper has fallen on tough times, and the editor is looking for a human-interest story that might increase circulation. Without an increase in subscriptions, the paper is scheduled to fold in six months. The pressure is on the editor, and Mo becomes the scapegoat for the paper's rise or fall. The editor is counting on her story to provide a lifeline for the paper, for him, and for the community.

"Where's Mo? I can never find her when I need her!" Ben screamed.

A frightened young coworker responded, "She hasn't come in yet."

"That's the second time this week she's been late."

Just as he turned to enter his office, Mo, young, bubbly, and freckled with short hair, entered the press room and approached him.

"Where have you been? I've been looking for you all morning!"

"I've been working on plans to spend time with my family in Coulton for the holidays," I replied.

"That's a poor excuse. Your job comes before your family. In my office. Now!"

Ben was good-hearted but under a lot of pressure to keep the paper afloat. He had absorbed the stress but recently began having chest pains. He was overweight, didn't exercise, and ate unhealthily. His poor lifestyle was a strong indicator that his job was adversely affecting his health. His doctor had advised him to take time off, but he ignored the recommendation. The paper's circulation had been decreasing for two years, and the owners' ultimatum to increase circulation had become a stark reality.

I entered Ben's office, and he told me to take a seat. I realized something was up, and the thought of being fired entered my mind. He sat behind his desk, opened the front drawer, and popped a pill. A few minutes passed, and then he finally looked at me. I thought, *Here it comes. I'll be pounding the pavement in the morning.*

"Mo, I need you to help me figure out a way to improve circulation," he said.

Relieved, I asked, "Do you have any ideas?"

"I have one," he responded. "Tell me a little bit about your family history and living in Coulton."

Mo began telling him what she knew, which was little.

"Can you be more specific? Tell me about your life growing up in poverty and living in a small Eastern Kentucky coal town. I'm also interested in the town's culture and whether it has changed since its settlement. Do you know anything about the town's history?"

"I'm not familiar with my family history or the town's settlement, but my grandmother and mother would know a lot."

"Do you think they would mind telling you what they know?" he asked.

"Some of it might be personal and difficult for them to tell, I said, "but I think they would like to tell as much as they know about our family story and previous generations."

Ben sat back in his chair and looked at me. "How would you like to take a few weeks during the holidays and interview members of your family, friends, and some of the townspeople? I would like you to write about your family's stories, the culture they found when they first came to Coulton, and how they adapted to the differences between their Scottish home and new home," he said.

I scrutinized Ben's facial expression to see if he was serious. "Why do you think my family story would help circulation?"

"I think our readers would be interested in a story that describes the early families that settled in Kentucky," he replied.

"How would you market the story?"

"We'd start with an advanced promo in the Sunday paper informing readers about the article, the timeline for its publication, and how it would be circulated. We'd also provide brief snippets to gain their interest."

I had so many questions I wanted to ask but couldn't put them in the right context. I recognized that the make-or-break story could influence the paper's life and my future as a journalist. But I simply asked, "Why me?"

"Because you're a talented writer, and your story could be the answer to our problem."

"Can I think about it for a couple of days?" I asked.

"Yes," Ben said.

I got up from my chair, turned, and walked toward the door. I went to my desk, where I sat for a long time thinking about Ben's request.

Friday afternoon passed slowly. I thought it would never end. I got to my apartment and called my mother immediately. She answered quickly, and I explained the assignment. She listened but didn't say much. I wondered if she thought our family story would reveal skeletons in our family closet.

I ended the call and sat on a chair next to the kitchen window, watching a bird fly from tree to tree. I assumed he was trying to decide which branch to perch on. As I got ready for bed, I thought about the bird I had seen earlier and compared its indecision with my dilemma. I realized my decision would determine the paper's future, and my career was now in my hands. My body trembled, and I feared that I wouldn't succeed.

I fell asleep and woke up an uncountable number of times, worried about making the right decision. I had two days before returning to work, and I tried to stay busy without thinking about my options. On Sunday evening, I had finally come to a decision. I would do it!

I got to the office early, knowing that Ben always arrived an hour before me. I knocked on his door, and he waved me in.

"Sit down," he said.

I sat and quickly said, "I've decided to take you up on your offer."

Ben looked at me with a full-face smile and said, "I thought you would. Let me know your plan, and I'll begin marketing and advertising in our next Sunday edition."

I left Ben's office relieved that I had made the decision but worried about its outcome.

It was mid-November, and my plan was to spend the Thanksgiving, Christmas, and the New Year holidays interviewing and editing and have the story ready for publication by the end of January. I sent an email to Ben and called my mother to tell her about my plan. Both responded positively. I left Lexington on November 20 and planned to return to the *Gazette* the second week of January.

CHAPTER 3
HOME FOR THE HOLIDAYS

I ARRIVED AT MY BIRTH HOME late Saturday afternoon. Mom welcomed me with open arms, and Granny followed suit. When I walked down the entry hallway and smelled a familiar aroma coming from the kitchen, I knew Mom had made my favorite country dinner fried chicken, collard greens, mashed potatoes, and homemade biscuits. I was also certain she had baked an apple pie.

I climbed the stairs to my bedroom, opened the door, and saw that nothing had changed. My childhood dolls were placed carefully on my bed, and my teenage possessions were in full view on my dresser and walls. I unpacked quickly because I knew Mom would have supper on the table at exactly five o'clock. I wasn't wrong. I heard her familiar voice calling from the stairwell right on time.

I hurried down the stairs and sat down in the chair that I had used for more than twenty years. Mom and Granny sat in their usual seats. The chair at the head of the table remained vacant. Daddy had passed two years ago, the same month I graduated from Morehead State University.

I remembered that day vividly. I got a call from Mom telling me that Daddy had had a heart attack and died. She was crying hard and could hardly tell me what happened. I rushed home and consoled her and Granny the best I could. I was equally upset but was able to keep my composure. We planned Daddy's funeral and celebration. He was buried in the Coulton cemetery next to the rest of the Healy family. The townspeople joined us during that sad time and helped us get through the tragedy.

I spent a week with Mom and Granny until I felt they could manage without me. Then I returned to Lexington and prepared for job interviews. I thought of Daddy and how proud he was of me for going to college and graduating. I missed him.

Daddy was exceptionally proud of me because I was the only child in the family to go to college and graduate. He was equally proud because I had earned an academic scholarship and graduated cum laude with a degree in journalism.

I snapped out of my funk and glanced at Mom and Granny, who sat staring at me. Granny led us in prayer—a Healy custom that has been handed down from generation to generation. When she finished, I eagerly dove into the country-style bowls placed in the center of the table. Mom suggested we have dessert in the living room.

I hadn't mentioned the details of my work assignment because I wasn't certain how to approach it. I thought it might be a sensitive issue for Mom and Granny, and I wasn't sure they would like me to expose our family's story to the world. I finally decided to share my thoughts.

Without reservation, Mom and Granny supported the story. Mom recommended I interview Granny because she knew the family history and when and how our family had arrived in Kentucky. I looked at Granny and saw tears rolling down her cheeks, so I changed the subject and asked Mom questions about my friends and their families while we ate our apple pie à la mode. After dessert, I helped with the dishes and thought about questions to ask Granny in our interview.

Granny was eighty-three years old, but her memory was like a steel trap, and she had the energy of a spring chicken. She was the sixth and last child my great-grandmother had. She was born in 1940 and baptized Lisa Marie Healy. Great-Granny was forty years old when Granny was born. Granny said her birth was a complete surprise.

After we finished our dessert, I asked Granny when she would like to begin her interview. She was watching TV but turned her head toward me and asked, "When do you want to start?"

"How's Monday morning?" I suggested, and she agreed.

Sunday was devoted to church and meeting old friends—and the possibility of bumping into Bobbie Joe, my high school flame. Granny and I woke up at about the same time on Sunday morning. I'm certain the smell of biscuits and gravy had something to do with it. After breakfast, we drove to the Coulton Baptist Church, where our family had attended "Bible Belt" services for more than fifty years. Religion was an essential part of our culture. We firmly believed that if we obeyed the Ten Commandments faithfully, we would live eternally thereafter.

We were greeted at the front door by Pastor Sully. I noticed a number of my high school friends and Bobbie Joe were seated in the front pew. I listened attentively to Pastor Sully's sermon that emphasized the determination that Jesus had in spreading God's word. I connected the sermon with the zeal that I had for my new challenge.

After church, I met up with my friends and noticed that Bobby Joe wasn't with them. I thought our uncomfortable goodbye six years ago might be the reason. I had thought about him occasionally while attending college and while working for the paper but hadn't made an effort to see him, even during college breaks and work vacations. Mom mentioned often over the years that he worked in the mine and emphasized that he wasn't married. I was sure we would meet up during the next six weeks.

The church service ended, and we gathered in the fellowship hall to meet with the other parishioners. Afterward, we took the scenic route back home, and Mom and Granny talked about our new neighbors, births, deaths, and other changes since my last visit. To me, nothing had changed. Coulton was Coulton.

When we got home, we fixed a traditional Sunday afternoon dinner. When dinner was finished, we sat in the living room and talked about my brothers, sister, nieces, and nephews. Our extended family was large but not always close. Willie and Paul lived in Coulton, but Katy and John had moved north for better jobs and a better lifestyle.

After Mom and Granny had gone to bed, I sat for a while thinking about the newspaper story and Bobby Joe. It was late, and I decided to get a good night's sleep. I wanted to be at my best for my early morning interview with Granny.

CHAPTER 4
GREAT-GRANNY'S STORY (PART I)

I WOKE UP LATE AND KNEW Granny would be waiting for me. When I walked into the kitchen, I saw her sitting at the table dressed in her Sunday best. I poured a cup of coffee and sat down next to her. She looked at me with her piercing, deep blue eyes.

"I've been thinking we should begin our family story when your great-grandmother and great-grandfather decided to come to America. Mama started telling me her story when I was six years old. She told me about living in Scotland, her journey to America, traveling to Kentucky, and living in Coulton."

"That would be a great start," I said.

Granny's accent was a mix between a slight southern drawl and a Scottish brogue. Since Great-Granny and Great-Granddaddy weren't early settlers, they didn't have the Appalachian accent that previous generations had acquired over the past two hundred years. The evolution of the English language and Southern dialect intrigued me, and I hoped to find a place in the book to write about them.

I decided to write Granny's story about her mother exactly the way she told it to me. I thought using her grammar and wording would offer more credibility for the paper's readers. I wanted the newspaper article to be written with authenticity and use the language in which it was told. I was ready and armed with a couple of pencils and paper.

Granny looked at me and said, "Before I begin, I want to mention that Mama started telling me her life stories when I was six years old and continued until I was fifteen. She stopped suddenly each time, and I've always wondered why."

And then she began.

Mama told me she wasn't happy about being forced to get married to an older man she didn't know, and she definitely didn't want to go to America. Mama was kindhearted and would help anyone. She was strong-willed and determined to fight any problem that came along.

Before coming to America, she lived a happy life on her parents' farm and loved the Scottish village she grew up in. She helped grow potatoes and make honey. She often said the best part of her life was working on the farm, playing with her friends, and liking a simple life with her family.

Mama would talk to me for hours about how hard farm work was when she was younger, but when she reached her teens, she was able to work in the fields just like her mama, daddy, brothers, and sisters. I re-

member one story when she fell asleep in the potato patch and wasn't found till dark. Her mama and daddy thought she had run away because the work was so hard.

She had a few friends that she went to school with. They was farm kids that worked as hard as her. For fun, they would play hide and seek, hike, and fish. They only went to the village school till they were twelve. The villagers thought that was enough schooling for anyone.

Her dog, Mickie, was her best friend. She said she played with him every day and felt he understood every word she said. Mickie would go to the fields with her and sleep in her bed. When he died, Mama said she cried for days. Daddy wanted to get her a new one, but Mickie was the one and only dog for her.

Mama had three sisters and three brothers that was all older. She was born last. Her sisters took care of her as she was growing up. Her mama was always in the fields and didn't pay much attention to her. She often told me her mama was tired of having so many kids.

Church was the main thing in the villagers' lives. Mama's religion was Protestant. They went to the Presbyterian church and had a pastor who was strict and told sermons that scared her. She was afraid she would end up in hell if she did bad things. She believed in another life after she died. The villagers were God-fearing and lived by the Ten Commandments. Anyone who didn't follow the church rules was looked down on and was led by the devil. That belief has followed our family and the townspeople till today.

It was a village custom that girls get married young and have lots of babies, so when Mama was fifteen, her daddy decided she should get married. An older farm boy wanted to marry her, and Pastor Sully told Mama about the boy. Despite Mama's protests about marrying a man ten years older, the marriage was put together quickly, and Mama and Daddy was married in the small village Presbyterian church on April 15, 1925. Mama said she only knew Daddy for a couple of weeks.

They lived in a house on her daddy's farm for two months till Daddy decided to go to America. Mama said he was a strong and hardworking man. He didn't talk much and kept to himself. She said he treated her nice till he had too much to drink. Then he would yell and treat her like a child. She thought that was the way marriage was, especially since Daddy was helping her grow up.

In Scotland, Daddy was a successful farmer who paid Mama's parents handsomely for her hand. His family had a sheep farm and grew hay. He had worked on the farm since he was ten. Mama said he was tall and good-looking with big hands. When Daddy told Mama that they was going to America, she thought he would do farming.

But Daddy had his sights on going to America to seek his fortune and leave the problems that many families in Scotland faced during the 1920s. Poverty was everywhere, religion was forced on many, crime was bad, taxes was high, and politicians was crooked. Daddy saw America as an opportunity to start a new life with his young wife with a child on the way. He heard that after WWI, America had jobs and a lot of people from Scotland decided to leave and follow in the footsteps of the early settlers.

Three months after they was married, Daddy came in from the potato fields and told Mama they was leaving for America in a week. Mama said she was shocked and couldn't imagine leaving her family, friends, and a life she loved. She tried to talk Daddy out of going, but once he made a final decision about anything, there was no way of talking him out of it.

Mama said he was as stubborn as a mule. She was scared, about to have her first child, and would be far away from all that she ever knew.

After Daddy decided they were going to America, he told Mama about his plan. Mama told it this way. The first task Daddy had was to find a ship he could afford. The cheapest one was aboard a cargo ship. Daddy realized the journey would be difficult, but he couldn't afford the cost of a passenger ship. He got the ship tickets, and Mama and Daddy left Scotland seven days later. Daddy had gotten all the necessary papers needed for Mama and him to go to America. Mama said her mama, daddy, and all the children were at the port when the ship left. Mama waved goodbye from the ship with tears streaming down her cheeks.

Mama said she cried herself to sleep for the first few nights and dreamed of her friends and family. She hardly saw Daddy once they got on the ship. He was busy talking to people and making plans for when they got to America.

The ship left port on June 20, 1925. Traveling from Scotland to New York City was hard. The trip was supposed to take between six and eight days, but the weather and the route often determined how long the journey would take. Mama said the weather was bad at times. The sea was rough, food became scarce, and sickness and death occurred every day. Because Mama was pregnant, she was sick throughout the journey and always in need of food and water. Daddy would steal from other passengers to make sure Mama would survive and give birth.

Mama said life on the cargo ship was horrible. Passengers were crowded together, sick, hungry, and dirty. There was rats running everywhere. Fights happened a lot because of the poor conditions and the need to steal from one another. One time Daddy got into a fight stealing food for her and was stabbed in the stomach. His wound became infected, and he almost died. Another passenger from Scotland took care of him. She cleaned his wound every day and made sure that the infection didn't get worse. After the woman saved Daddy's life, they never saw her again.

During the journey, Mama said she grew to respect Daddy and began to dream about her new life in America. But even though Daddy cared for her, she always had a feeling that he was hiding something from her.

Despite all the hardships, they arrived at the Port of New York ten days after they left Scotland. It was a sunny and warm late June afternoon when the US Butterfield entered the port and unloaded its passengers. Mama often described the scene of the passengers getting off the ship and their eagerness to experience their new home. They seemed excited, even though they knew nothing about what was ahead of them. Neither did she. She said she was excited too and encouraged Daddy to share his future plans. He would ignore her requests because he had no plans.

Granny had been telling her mother's story for more than an hour and seemed eager to tell more. I encouraged her to take a break, which she eventually agreed to do. I was shocked by how much she remembered. I had heard bits and pieces of her parents' journey to America but never to the depth presented, and I began to think that there might be something to Ben's vision to save the newspaper. I had taken notes while Granny was telling Great-Granny's story and was anxious to learn what happened after her parents left the ship.

Granny returned fifteen minutes later with a glass of water and a willingness to continue telling her mama's story. I decided to ask a few questions to clarify parts of her story, adamant about making sure that all facts were relevant and interesting to the newspaper's readers. It was my responsibility to ensure that the story would be exciting enough to read from Sunday to Sunday for four weeks.

I asked Granny if her mother had relatives and friends on the ship. She said that her cousin Kate and her husband Patrick were constant companions, and they talked excitedly about their new venture. They planned to move together and find a place to live and raise their families.

"Did your mother ever express her true feelings about leaving Scotland, her parents, and her siblings?" I asked.

"She was homesick throughout the journey but looked forward to a new life in a new place with a brand-new child," Granny replied.

"Are you ready to continue the story?"

"I sure am," she said.

After Mama and Daddy got off the ship, they met up with Mama's cousin Kate and her husband Patrick. Mama said they stood there with no plans. She asked Daddy where they would live, what work he could get, and how they would travel to their destination. Daddy told Mama he met a fellow who was going to Kentucky, and he might be able to help. The man said a lot of Irish and Scottish families had settled in Kentucky as far back as the early 1800s and that might be a good place to live. He said that it was a thousand miles away and coal miners were needed in the mines. Daddy was a farmer, coal mining being something he knew nothing about, but Daddy and Patrick decided to go. Daddy had heard that a lot of Scottish families lived in a town called Coulton. He felt it would be good to be with people from Scotland who were the original settlers. He didn't know anything about Kentucky and its culture, but when they got there, he soon found out.

Mama said there was one big problem. How would they get there? Trains went to Kentucky, but the journey was hard and cost a lot of money. Cars and trucks were possibilities, but Daddy and Patrick had no money to buy one—and neither had ever drove one. With the little money Daddy and Mama had, they decided to take a train and get as close as possible to Kentucky. Once they got there, the plan was to buy a buckboard wagon and two horses and travel to the coal-mining town. The fellow who told Daddy about Kentucky said the new mines were in Harlan County and some of the miners lived in Coulton.

Mama, Daddy, her cousin, and her cousin's husband found a room for the night next to the train station. The train was leaving for Washington, DC at six in the morning. Mama said Daddy didn't sleep the whole night because he was afraid they would miss the train. They got to the station on time and began their journey to the unknown.

Two hours had passed since Granny started telling her mother's story. She described it with animation and color. I hoped that I could capture her presentation in writing. She continued to tell me what she knew about the first few months of her mama and daddy's marriage. She explained that it wasn't easy living with her daddy. He rarely talked and was always in a bad mood. Mama didn't know what was bothering him and always thought she was the problem. She said she tried to get him to talk, but he just ignored her. I thought the description of Granddaddy's personality was insightful and hoped it might lead to more information about what troubled him. I wanted to learn more about my great-grandparents' experiences while on the ship, so I asked Granny if she could tell me more. She continued with a detailed description of the cargo ship journey.

Mama was scared most of the time and worried about her baby. She didn't sleep well and was always hungry, and Daddy did the best he could to make sure she had food. Her memories about home kept her going from day to day. The thought that they would settle in Kentucky was beyond her imagination. She didn't know what to expect.

Mama told me about some of the passengers. There was more men than women and some children. The men and women would gather separately and talk about Scotland, their new home, and future plans. She overheard some women telling stories that were similar to hers. They talked about how they missed home, their fear of the unknown, and survival. Listening to their stories made Mama realize her feelings were no different from theirs.

Granny talked about the ship experience for almost an hour. I thought she might be tired, but she was in full stride and hadn't yet reached her peak. I suggested taking a break and continuing tomorrow, and she reluctantly agreed.

I left her and decided to review my notes and edit what I had written—a written piece is never finished and can always be written better. I had to keep my reading audience in mind and, more importantly, tell a story that would be interesting and hold their attention. My major concern was the make-or-break importance of crafting a story that had enough value to increase the newspaper's circulation. The pressure was more than I imagined. Only time would tell if it would work. I hoped for the best.

I needed a break and decided that meeting up with a few of my high school friends would relieve some of my stress. My best friend Sally agreed to meet me at the Horseshoe Tavern at eight o'clock. The tavern had a well-known history, complete with weekend brawls, hostile mine labor meetings, and non-church weddings, all of which added to the mountain culture.

Excited about meeting my friends and looking forward to seeing Bobbie Joe again, I laid out my finest country outfit and prepared for a night in the town. When I arrived at the tavern, I immediately bumped into Bobbie Joe. I was so embarrassed that I didn't say a word and walked straight to the bar where Sally Mae sat. A few of our friends joined us, and before long, we were shooting pool, dancing to George Strait, and carrying on like teenagers. The night flew by, and I said my goodbyes before heading to my car. This time I didn't bump into Bobbie Joe. He bumped into me.

We had been a steady couple in high school and often talked about a future together. He was my "first," and it made sense that we would settle in the valley, raise a flock of children, and live happily ever after. My acceptance and scholarship to Morehead University changed all that. The day I left for college was the last time we were together. I had often thought about Bobbie Joe while at school and during the two years I worked in Lexington. I dated a few guys and had an intimate relationship with one, but none of them could ever replace Bobbie Joe.

He looked me straight in the eyes and asked, "What do you have planned for the rest of the evening?"

I didn't know what to say. I certainly wasn't the type of person not to have a response to a question. *But this was Bobbie Joe.*

"Would you like to take a walk and catch up?" he asked.

I finally came to my senses and said, "That would be great."

The town park was a quick walk from the tavern, and it was a beautiful moonlit night. We walked silently for a while and came to a bench that overlooked Coulton Creek, where we sat and talked for more than an hour. Bobbie explained that he had been working in the mine for the past six years and had been promoted to supervisor a brief time ago. He hadn't married but had dated a couple of the locals, all of whom I was familiar with and would have to say were not Bobbie Joe's "type."

I told him about college life, my job, and the reason I was back home. He asked if I had a boyfriend back in Lexington. His question puzzled me. Did he still have feelings for me? Was there a chance for us to be together again? I hoped that I had not made a mistake in accepting Bobbie Joe's invitation and decided it was time to leave. We got up and walked to my car.

"Would you mind if I called you?" he asked.

I was still confused but said, "No, I wouldn't mind."

When I got home, I got ready for bed. I lay down and began thinking about my assignment and Bobbie Joe.

The next morning, I woke up early to the smell of cinnamon rolls and coffee. Mom and Granny were sitting at the kitchen table. Granny was dressed in her Sunday best again, waiting to begin the interview. I said good morning, poured a cup of coffee, and devoured a warm cinnamon roll. We talked about my night out and the fun I had with my high school friends. I didn't mention that I had spoken to Bobbie Joe.

Mom and Granny knew that I had been quite smitten with him in high school and that going to college and choosing to work in Lexington had interfered with marrying Bobbie, living in Coulton, and raising a large family. I knew they were disappointed by my life choices and career decisions and hoped that the Coulton story would be a hit and relieve some of their disappointment.

I looked at Granny and noticed she was a bit edgy. I knew she wanted to get started and probably didn't sleep the entire night. As I finished my last bite of cinnamon roll, Granny said, "Let's get going!" then told me she would like to continue with her mama's story after she got off the ship. And that's where she began.

Mama and Daddy never rode on a train, nor did Kate and Patrick. The adventure was exciting until Mama got sick and threw up all over her seat. She was three weeks pregnant and had experienced morning sickness during the ship ride, but she thought it had passed. She threw up for two days, ate little, and slept a lot. On the third day, she felt a little better and was able to keep some food down.

When they reached Washington, DC, they settled in a hotel and waited two days for a train to Columbus, Ohio. Mama was feeling much better when they boarded the 7 a.m. train. It took five hours to get to Columbus, where they planned to stay at a hotel until the next morning's transfer train to Lexington, Kentucky.

Daddy bumped into a man at the hotel. Mama said the man was polite and accepted Daddy's apology. The next morning, they boarded the train and reached Lexington by noon. When they got to Lexington, Daddy reached into his pocket for his billfold. It was gone! Patrick had told him about pickpockets, but Daddy ignored him. Mama said the man Daddy bumped into might have stolen it. Fortunately, Mama had most of Daddy's money hidden in her shoe—she had learned about pickpocketing from a ship passenger.

They learned there was no trains to Harlan County and decided not to buy a wagon and team of horses because they didn't know what was ahead of them. Their final destination, Coulton, was still a hundred miles away, so they walked to the Greyhound station to check on a bus. There was a bus leaving for Harlan County that afternoon. They bought tickets and arrived in Coulton after a six-hour bus ride. Mama told me the ride from Lexington to Coulton was long.

Mama said the mountains and valleys in Kentucky were beautiful and the view was breathtaking. It reminded her of home. She was certain she would be happy there. When they reached the top of the mountain that overlooked Coulton, she noticed that the town was divided into three different housing sections. On the left side of town was a group of small, unkempt houses. On the opposite side was the larger and well-kept houses. In the valley between the two sides was a row of broken-down shanties that stretched up the hollow. The train track ran through the middle of the two different housing sections and stopped where the hollow began. Mama saw a small grocery store, a church, and a one-room schoolhouse next to the small houses. The opposite side of the tracks was different. There was a big grocery store, clothing shops, and a number of smaller stores. Mama questioned why the town was divided into three separate sections and learned that each section housed a separate group of people. The mine workers lived in the small houses on the left side of the tracks and the rich in the larger houses on the right side of the tracks. The Black people lived in the valley between the miners' and rich peoples' houses.

Mama said in Scotland everyone lived together, whether you was poor or rich. Of course, the rich owned more land and had bigger farms, but everyone got along without any problems. She was anxious to see if it was the same in her new home.

Granny had taken a break, and I was thinking about the three housing sections. I had learned about the class system early on and always thought that one day it would not exist. As I grew older, I realized that a caste system exists on all continents. There are those who have more, those who have less, and a majority who are stuck in the middle. In Coulton, the miners were in the middle. I now believed that the likelihood of eradicating the system was just a dream.

Granny returned to continue telling her mama's story. She sat comfortably in a chair next to a window. I realized that Great-Granny, Granny, my mother, and me were all cut from the same fabric—work hard, love your family, and trust in God.

I cleared my head and apologized to Granny for not listening. She hadn't skipped a beat and had continued telling her story while I was deep in thought. I hadn't heard anything she said, so I asked her if she would mind repeating what happened after Great-Granny realized she would be living in a town where families were divided by race and wealth. Granny continued telling her mother's story about living in Scotland and compared it to Coulton.

Mama said she had grown up in Scotland where all families lived the same. There was no separation between old Scottish families or people who moved to their small town. Except for the shopkeepers, most of the families were farmers. Those who had money had inherited it or earned it over gener-

ations of hard work. Mama said she was uncomfortable with the separations and had a tough time accepting them.

I asked Granny if the divisions had changed during her lifetime.

"The separation still existed when I was young. The rich continued to oversee the poor, and the mining company continued to control the miners who owned most of the land. The housing hasn't changed, and the three groups still get along. Over the years, there were times when arguments and fights broke out among the rich, miners, and Black people. I have a lot of disturbing stories to tell you about that," she said.

"How about we save those stories for when you tell me about growing up in Coulton," I replied.

As Granny spoke, I continued to be surprised that she remembered her mama's stories so vividly. It was as if she had written daily in a diary and had read it over before our interview. I sometimes wondered if Granny was adding a little extra storytelling of her own.

As I listened to Granny's story about her mother, I realized my great-grandmother was a pioneer woman. It took a lot of guts to leave her Scotland home with a husband who had been chosen for her and travel by ship, train, and bus to a town in a foreign country. I figured this was just the beginning of finding out who Great-Granny really was.

We took a short break, and when I entered the living room, Granny was there, ready to go.

"What took you so long?" she asked.

After seeing her new hometown from a distance, Mama said she was anxious to find out exactly how the housing separation worked. On the bus ride down the mountain, she saw a park next to a winding creek that led to the hollow between the two housing sections. She saw small gardens and green pastures surrounded by a huge mountain range and thought about the similarities between her new and old homes. The landscape of both was beautiful, welcoming, and safe. At that point, Mama thought that even though her new home could never replace her village in Scotland, she was going to give it a try.

When Mama, Daddy, Patrick, and Kate reached the center of town, the bus pulled into a station next to a small store. The sign above the door read, "Slate Mining Company Store." When they got off the bus, Mama looked around and saw the man Daddy had met at the New York port who told him about Harlan County and the mining jobs. Daddy approached him and they talked about working in the mines. The man, whose name was Mr. Jenson, said he worked for the Slate Mining Company and he would help Patrick and Daddy get jobs. He told Daddy there were no mines in Coulton, but the nearby town of Harlan had just opened a mine and needed workers. Daddy's worries about finding a job might have come to an end. Mama was still worried about where they would live, but Mr. Jenson told Daddy there was some houses in Coulton that miners and their families rented from the mining company. The only catch was you had to work for the company. When Daddy told Mama about the houses for the miners, she realized that the row of small houses on the left side of town would be her new home.

Daddy didn't know how long it would take to get a job, so he and Mama rented a room in a boarding house next to the bus station. Patrick and Kate tagged along.

The next morning, Daddy and Patrick met Mr. Jenson, and they took the coal train to Harlin. Daddy was introduced to the foreman, who asked questions about his mining experience. Because Daddy was a farmer and had no experience, the foreman wasn't going to hire him. But then Daddy described a farmer's work, and the foreman realized that a farmer's daily chores might be just as hard as mining. He gave Daddy and Patrick jobs, and they started the next day. Daddy took the coal train back to Coulton and told Mama the good news.

He had signed the papers to rent the mining company's house, was given a company grocery card, and received an upfront portion of his hourly pay. Mama always said that after paying the monthly rent and buying food, there wasn't much money left. Daddy soon found that he had become a company man and had lost the freedom he had as a farmer, something that he took for granted back home. He worked hard six days a week, ten hours a day. He would take the coal train to Harlin at six in the morning and return to Coulton at six in the evening. Mama said he would come home so tired he couldn't talk or eat. All he wanted to do was sleep.

The months passed quickly, and Mama was near term. The baby was due any day. The closest hospital was in Lexington, seventy miles from Coulton. Daddy had no way of getting to the hospital, so Mama had her first baby in a mine-owned three-room house with no heat or indoor plumbing. A local midwife and Kate helped, and Mama's first of six children was born healthy on December 28, 1925.

Daddy celebrated with Patrick and Kate. They had taken a likin' to moonshine and folk music—Daddy was familiar with the homemade whiskey that the original Irish and Scottish settlers brought to America. Neighbors joined the celebration of birth, dancing and singing around a bonfire. Mama said it was a happy time. They named their first child Mary Lou.

Over the next fifteen years, five more children was born. I was the last, born in 1940, and named Lisa Marie. I was born the same year Daddy died. He was forty years old and died from black lung disease.

Before he died, they had moved from the three-room house to a bigger house with three bedrooms but still no heat or indoor plumbing. Mama knew Daddy had a lung disease, and coal mining made it worse. When Daddy died, Mary Lou was fifteen and my three brothers ranged in age from four to thirteen. To help Mama, Mary Lou found odd jobs, but they weren't much help in paying the rent and buying food. Mama had saved some money, and Mary Lou later got a job at the mine office, and the money helped a little. Timmy got a job as a gardener for a rich family. Daddy's life insurance policy was a godsend and helped Mama keep the new house and provide for us. I remember Mama saying that Daddy had worked hard to get life insurance for all the miners. She said she struggled at times, but we all grew to adulthood living in Coulton and working for the mining company

Granny paused for a couple of minutes and wiped tears from her eyes. Then she regained her composure and continued.

Despite knowing about Daddy's disease and dealing with his difficult personality, Mama said she was heartbroken when he died. There was a funeral at the Baptist church, and Daddy was buried under an old elm tree. The townspeople were supportive and helped her get through it all. After the funeral and burial, there was a celebration of Daddy's life. Neighbors brought food and drinks, and kind words were said about him. Mama said Daddy was very popular with the miners and tried to start a union so they could make more money and get better working conditions. The miners were grateful for his help and appreciated all he did.

Mama said no celebration was had without the mountain drink. Moonshine-making had been handed down from previous generations and became the customary drink for celebrations. Stills were located in the hills, and 'shine was always available for special occasions. Daddy was considered one of the boys and often drank with his friends. On more than one occasion, Daddy drank too much and got into a fight. During his funeral celebration, however, all the men were respectful and on their best behavior.

After Daddy died, Mama got a job at the company store and Mary Lou looked after us. While growing up, I became overly attached to my big sister. A memory that still stays with me is her death. It was 1955, and I had just turned fifteen when she died in a fire at one of the mining company's buildings. She was thirty years old. I was grateful for all she did for me. I missed her terribly and always wished she could have been there for me for the rest of my teen years and as I got older. After Mary Lou died, Mama was able to keep the house because she worked in the company store. She stopped telling me her life stories after Mary Lou's death. I think she started spending more time with me because she knew how close I had been to my sister. I started sharing my thoughts and feelings with her, and she often gave me good advice about friendships, school, and boys.

Remember I told you Mama stopped telling me stories about her life when I was fifteen? That was the same year Mary Lou died. I'm not sure, but maybe that's why. I asked her a number of times why she stopped, but she never gave an answer. Another thing that I continued to question was why did she start telling me her stories when I was six?

"Would you like to take a break?" I asked.

"Yes," she said.

I sat back on the couch and thought about where we had left off and where to begin again. Great-Granny had stopped telling Granny her stories when she was fifteen-years old. Granny mentioned she might have stopped her stories because Mary Lou died. A traumatic experience often triggers an emotion that changes behavior. That might be the reason.

I realized that a lot of the family stories took place when Great-Granddaddy was alive, and I wanted to include them in Granny's story.

"Granny, can you recall any family or town stories that occurred *after* Granddaddy died?" I asked.

"Well, I don't remember much before I was five, but there was one time I've never forgotten," she said.

"Do you feel comfortable talking about it?" I asked.

"It was six years after Daddy died," she said. "Mama came home from the company store crying. She walked into the kitchen, sat down, laid her head on the table, and sobbed uncontrollably. I asked her what was wrong, and she didn't say anything. After a few minutes, she looked up at me and said, 'Patrick died!'"

That was also the time when Mama started telling me her life stories. "Do you think Patrick's death had anything to do with that?" I asked.

"It sounds like a good reason, but I'm not sure."

I had begun to put two and two together—Patrick's death was another trigger that influenced Great-Granny to start telling Granny her stories.

Patrick worked in the mines alongside Daddy until Daddy died. He died six years after Daddy. Patrick was Daddy's best friend, and he helped Mama a lot before and after Daddy died. Mama was really close to him. He was always there when she needed help and comfort.

Mama said one of the mine walls caved in, and he was crushed to death. I think she took Patrick's death harder than Daddy's. All the miners and their families felt the tragedy. Mama said she had met a few families from Scotland who gave her support after Daddy died, and they reached out to Kate. She was devastated and left to raise four children alone. She had no money saved, lost her company house, and moved to Lexington. Mama said Kate hated Coulton and everything about mountain life.

Although she was sad about Patrick's death, she was angry that the mining company couldn't care less about the families' who lost their loved ones in mining accidents. Mama decided to continue Daddy's work to help the miners. She organized a group of women and protested the lack of support for families when they lost a husband or relative in a mine accident. She challenged the mining company for three years until the company created a trust fund for family survivors. Mama continued to push the mining company to make improvements for the workers. She would talk about how the company took advantage of their employees—safety rules were weak, and if you was sick and couldn't work, you didn't get paid. There was no hospital or doctor's insurance. Mama's biggest complaint was how the company would take money out of Daddy's paycheck for groceries and house rent. She said that by the time Daddy brought his pay home every week, more than half of it was gone. Mama and Daddy never knew how much money he really made. They struggled from week to week, and as Mama had more kids, their lives became even more difficult.

By 1930, working conditions had gotten worse and families fell deeper into poverty. Angry miners and their families talked about a strike, and the next year, it happened. The men went on strike and protested outside the mine. There was a lot of fights about scabs coming in and taking jobs. There was an incident that Mama told me about where a miner was shot to death outside the mine for picketing and preventing scabs from taking their jobs. She said all the miners and their families were angry, and she and many other women would walk the picket line every day with their husbands. Mama took Mary Lou and Timmy with her when she walked the line—Mary Lou was six and Timmy was four. The miners were often thrown in jail because fights broke out every day. Mama said she went to jail once for punching a policeman and spent the night there with Mary Lou and Timmy until she borrowed the money to get out. The strike lasted for more than two years. Eventually, pay was increased, better working conditions were given, and health insurance was available for all families. Mama thought the biggest benefit of the strike was the closing of the company store. The new owners agreed to keep Mama on, and the mining company said she could keep renting the house. When the new grocer took over, the prices went down, and the food was better. She said everything wasn't perfect, but it was much improved.

Despite the troubled times, there were often good ones. There were parties, holiday celebrations, and many friendships. All the mining families was in the same boat and did the best they could. Entire families would get together on Saturday nights outside or in a big barn the mining company had built to house their equipment. Mama said she and Daddy would dance and sing for hours. She told me that one time Daddy got so drunk he passed out on the dance floor. Mama was so mad she kicked him and took Mary Lou and Timmy home. Daddy came home later and went right to bed. They never talked about it, but I'm sure Mama made him pay for it. I didn't realize back then, but all the good and tough times had started the beginning of a mountain culture that would be handed down from generation to generation. Even though all the mining families were poor, there was a bond and a pride in who they had become—hard working, caring, and thankful.

Granny paused and teared up but quickly started telling her mother's story again.

Daddy had worked hard, and after a few years he told Mama he believed he had made the right decision to come to America. He was proud that he had raised his family in Coulton, and his life with Mama added to the feeling. Mama often talked about how she was left with five children to support after he died. After I was born, she said she worked as hard as she could to make sure we grew up as healthy and happy as possible. As you know, I was the last of the brood, born in 1940, the same year Daddy died. He was only forty.

Mama died in 1970. She was seventy. Before she died, she told me she was worn out from raising us kids, trying to put food on the table, and dealing with the mining company. I think about Mama and the stories she told about Daddy a lot—both the good and bad times. Most of all, I think about how Mama worked so hard to raise my sister, brothers, and me. It always seemed as though she was lonely and searching for the life, she had left behind in Scotland. Her love for me and my siblings was obvious to us and her friends, and that love has been handed down from her generation to yours.

Mo, you are the end result of it all. Your story about our family and the mountain culture will be read by thousands, and they will get to know how life was back then and how it is now. I'm so proud of you.

Granny broke down in tears when she finished, and I followed suit. Her story was so heartbreaking that I was encouraged to continue and felt that the paper's readers would feel the same.

I spent the rest of the week rewriting, editing, and formatting the story. I wanted it to be perfect before I gave it to Ben. The weekend had snuck up on me, and I realized that all work and no play wasn't good medicine. I gave Sally Mae a call, and we met up at the tavern.

When I opened the tavern door and bumped into Bobbie Joe, my mind began to wander. Was he waiting for me, or was it just a coincidence he was there? Regardless, my true purpose for going to the tavern was met.

"I was looking for you," he said.

"How did you know I would be here," I asked.

"Sally Mae said you would be coming. Would you like to sit at the bar and have a drink?" he asked.

I wasn't expecting to run into Bobbie again so soon, but I agreed to a drink. We sat at the bar, and Bobbie ordered a beer, and I got a rum and coke. We didn't speak for the first couple of minutes, but then Bobbie finally broke the ice and asked how my work project was going. I explained that I was interviewing family, friends, and neighbors for a story about coal-mining families.

"Granny is my first family member interview, and I'm almost finished," I said.

"Do I qualify as a friend since I've known you since the second grade?" he asked.

"You certainly do."

"It would be my pleasure to be interviewed, Miss Reporter."

I had planned to use his story but hadn't yet asked his permission, so I changed the subject and talked instead about high school, his family, and his job. We sat at the bar for over an hour and talked about everything important to us—except "us."

We decided to take a walk along the creek. It felt different being with Bobbie Joe this time. I felt comfortable. We sat down on the same bench we'd sat on last week, and he put his arm around me, then leaned toward me and kissed me. I responded willingly.

"Would you like to go to Lexington next Saturday and take in a movie and have dinner?" he asked.

"There's a movie I'd like to see, and I'd like to take you to one of my favorite restaurants," I said.

"Great! I'll call you midweek to talk about the plan."

We walked back to the tavern, Bobbie kissed me goodbye, and I met up with Sally Mae and our friends.

"You're late," said Sally. "You don't have to explain. I saw you and Bobbie Joe at the bar."

I had another drink and danced to country music for the rest of the night—but my heart pounded whenever I thought of Bobbie Joe.

I had been home for a week and was excited about the story I was writing. I thought Granny's story about my great-grandparents was interesting, but it didn't quite have the impact I was looking for, so I wanted to dive into the nitty gritty of their personal lives. I just had a feeling that the true story had not been told yet.

On Thursday evening, I got the expected call from Bobbie Joe. "Are you still up for a trip this weekend?" he asked.

"Yes, what are the plans?"

"How about I pick you up Saturday around two o'clock, and we'll head to Lexington to have supper and see a movie. We should be back before midnight."

"Sounds good, but remember that I want to take you to one of my favorite restaurants," I said.

I put down my phone and lay down on my bed, planning to take only a short nap, but I woke up two hours later. While I slept, I dreamed about my story and, of course, Bobbie Joe.

Mom and Granny were fixing supper. Mama looked at me when I walked into the kitchen and said, "I'm glad you're up. I want to talk to you about Thanksgiving and Christmas. Your brother Willie wants to have Thanksgiving dinner at his house this year. Is that okay with you?" she asked.

"Sounds good," I said. "What about Christmas?"

"We will have most of the family here," she replied.

We sat down for supper, and I asked Granny if she would like to tell me more about her mama's story. With her head tilted down toward her plate, she said, "I've pretty much told you all of Mama's story. My story after Daddy died is a story in itself."

"I figured that, and I want to write it separately from your mama's story. Are you sure that you've finished with that one?"

Granny didn't respond immediately and had a sheepish look on her face.

"Is there something you're not telling me?" I felt like she was hiding something, but I pushed those thoughts aside and decided to begin writing Granny's story after my weekend date with Bobbie Joe.

Bobbie Joe picked me up promptly at two on Saturday, and we headed to Lexington around four thirty. It was too early for supper, and the movie didn't start until eight, so we walked around the mall for an hour until we agreed that it was time to eat.

"Okay, what's the name of the restaurant you wanted to take me to?" he asked.

I was a bit reluctant to tell him because I didn't know if he liked Chinese food. There were no Asian restaurants in Coulton, and I thought it likely that he had never been to one, but I finally said, "Egg Fu Yung."

Bobbie Joe looked at me and laughed.

"Why are you laughing?" I asked.

"Because that's my favorite restaurant in Lexington."

I joined him in laughter, and we drove off to the restaurant. I was surprised that he liked Chinese and even more shocked that he knew how to use chopsticks. I wondered if more surprises were in store.

By the time we finished eating, it was seven thirty.

"What movie did you decide on?" he asked.

"I just finished reading a book called *Hillbilly Elegy*, and the movie is playing at the Grand," I said.

Bobbie Joe didn't comment. He drove to the theater and bought tickets. We sat in the middle row surrounded by an unusual-looking group—country people loaded down with popcorn, sodas, and candy. What intrigued me the most was their dress. Most of them were in their twenties. The boys wore white shirts and ties, and the girls wore dresses or skirts.

I leaned toward Bobbie Joe and asked if he noticed the clothes the moviegoers were wearing. He and I were just wearing jeans and sweaters.

"Looks like their Sunday best. They're from small towns and don't go out much, so this was a special occasion and they dressed appropriately," he said.

I thought it was more than that, and their attendance at this particular movie and their dress had to do with the subject matter of the movie. I hadn't told Bobbie Joe what the movie was about because I wanted his unbiased opinion when it was over. We watched the movie intently, and I often glanced at the other viewers to see their reactions to certain parts.

When the movie ended, we walked to Bobbie Joe's car. He had been silent until then. When we got settled inside, he looked at me and asked if I thought that the story was similar to his family story. I hadn't thought about it, but I had to admit that it was in some ways.

Bobbie Joe's family was poor and had worked in the mines since their arrival in Coulton. He had traced his family heritage back to 1820. He lived in a part of Coulton where the original settlers had first migrated. His life was similar to mine—we went to the same schools, our parents worked in the mines, and we were poor. The only difference between us was that I had left Coulton and started a new life. Bobbie Joe had stayed in Coulton, and he worked at the mine like all his family. He didn't aspire to anything more than that.

A few minutes passed before Bobbie Joe asked if I had taken him to see the movie so he could see himself in the main character. The biggest difference between Bobbie Joe and JD Vance, the lead character, was that JD escaped and broke the chain of poverty that had bound his family from generation to generation. My intention was not to embarrass Bobbie Joe or motivate him to change, and I hoped he didn't see it that way.

He remained quiet on the way home. When we were halfway there, I asked him if he was upset with me.

"No, but the movie brought up issues that have been bothering me for years," he said.

"Would you like to talk about it?" I asked.

He didn't answer, and we drove the rest of the way without talking. Before I got out of the car at my house, I asked if he would like to see me tomorrow.

"Yes," he said. "I'll see you at church."

CHAPTER 5
BOBBIE JOE'S STORY

I woke up early and thought about Bobbie Joe immediately. I was happy that I had told him I would see him after church. I thought about his family and realized I didn't know much.

Bobbie Joe and I had met in grade school, and we continued our schooling together through high school. We had an unusual relationship during high school. We went to school functions—football and basketball games, school dances—with each other a number of times. I couldn't say we were boyfriend and girlfriend, but I did let him kiss me once after a school dance. In our senior year, I didn't see much of him. He participated in sports, and I was busy applying to colleges. We didn't see each other the summer before I went away to college, so we never said goodbye. During my college years and the two years I worked in Lexington, I rarely thought about him, but the surprise "bump" at the tavern when I first got home opened a door that I had unconsciously closed long ago. I wondered if the door might open wider and lead to a future relationship.

Mama walked into the kitchen just as I was flouring the chicken I was about to fry.

"What's with the cooking?" she asked.

"I'm meeting Bobbie Joe after church and decided we would have a picnic by the creek," I replied.

She looked at me with an approving smile. "Sounds great. I hope you enjoy yourselves. It certainly would be nice if the two of you could connect after all these years."

Mama had secretly hoped that Bobbie Joe and I would get married, have a bunch of kids, and live in Coulton. My future was way beyond her dream.

When I left church, Bobbie Joe was waiting for me. He smiled and didn't show any signs of being upset about our date or the movie. He greeted me with a broad smile and asked what I had planned.

"Wait a minute—I have to get something from the car," I said and came back with a picnic basket draped over my arm.

"What's with the basket?"

"I thought we could have lunch by the creek."

Bobbie Joe gave his customary nod, and we walked to the creek.

It was a gorgeous fall day. The autumn leaves had turned and had begun to float to the ground. Bobbie Joe found a beautiful spot under a huge oak tree. I spread a blanket on the ground and opened the basket. He looked at me and asked if we could talk for a few minutes before we ate. The few minutes turned into an hour. He started the conversation with an apology.

"I regret the way I acted after the movie last night," he said. "I'm afraid the movie struck a nerve and brought up something I've been feeling since I was in grade school."

"Would you like to talk about it?" I asked.

"It's a long and personal story that I've never told. I'm not sure you'd want to hear it or understand how it has affected me for so many years."

"Try me."

"I don't know where to begin because my family history plays a big role in how I feel."

"Well, why don't you share your feelings first? Then you can trace them back to the issues," I suggested.

"I think that'll work," Bobbie Joe said. "A number of things have bothered me for a long time. The stories about the original settlers in 1820 haunt me. And I don't like the negative perception that outsiders have about mountain people. They're stereotyped as isolated, uncouth, and warmongers, and that stereotype has been handed down to my generation."

"Outsiders have publicized that view for years," I said.

"I know that mountain culture has changed, and the early settlers' descriptions don't exist anymore, but the public still believes it. Even worse, I can't rid myself of that perception," he said.

"That's some pretty heavy baggage to be carrying for all these years. Let's start with the perception outsiders have about us," I said.

Okay, the thing that irritates me a lot is the labeling—rednecks, hillbillies, and white trash, to name a few. I've been hearing these negative descriptions all my life, and they aren't true. They imply that all mountain people are stupid, ignorant, and dependent on government poverty programs to survive. That might be true for a small percentage, but most of us are smart, industrious, hardworking, and God-fearing. Now, we might be conservative, set in our ways, stubborn, and isolated from the mainstream, but that has nothing to do with our intelligence. I know there's a belief that we are moonshine alcoholics, weed smokers, and a violent lot, but again, that only applies to a small percentage of the mountain population. Stories about incest and illegitimate children disturb me the most. The century-old tale about the Hatfield-McCoy feud over a stolen pig has been so misinterpreted and embellished by outsiders that they believe we are all descendants of those families. Movies and books continue to portray mountain families as gun-toting, racist, and insensitive, when in reality, we're peaceful unless there's cause not to be, have a strong family bond, are more than willing to help our neighbors, and enjoy celebrations, music, and the arts. The white supremacist movement has added another negative layer to the cultural misconception outsiders have. And there's an entirely different story regarding the mining companies and politicians that I'll save for another day. Last but not least, the perception that our language isn't American because of our accent bothers me. I'll tell you that mountain people are the most patriotic group in this country. Who do you think were among the first to participate in WWII, the Korean War, the Vietnam War, and the Middle Eastern wars?

Bobbie Joe took a breath and paused for a minute, giving me the opportunity to jump in.

"Wow, you've built up some heavy guilt in twenty-six years. Have you been exposed to all that personally, or have generational stories influenced your feelings?" I asked.

"I think what I feel has been mostly secondhand. I heard stories from my grandparents and parents that have influenced how I feel."

"Is there more you would like to talk about?" I asked.

"I think so . . ."

"How about we take a break and have lunch?" I said. "I was up early this morning to fix this meal, you know."

"What's on the menu?"

"Fried chicken, baked okra, homemade biscuits, and apple pie for dessert!"

We talked a little as we ate, but not as heavily as we had earlier. Once finished, we cleaned up and stretched out on the blanket, looking up at the clear blue sky, scattered white clouds, and the occasional bird that flew by overhead in its freedom flight. It was a peaceful setting. After an hour had passed, Bobbie Joe asked if I would like to hear more of his story, and I nodded.

As I said, I have never told anyone about my feelings. I realize I told you a lot earlier, more than you wanted to hear, and I want to thank you for listening.

Another thing that has bothered me since high school is the idea that I was destined to live in Coulton, work in the mine, get married, and have a bunch of kids. That's what every member of my family has done since settling here in the 1900s. But I want more than that. I want to go to college, leave Coulton forever, and get a decent job, but my family history haunts me. I always wanted to be an engineer and build bridges or roads, but the negative opinion I have of myself and the fact that I have no money or role models haunts me. I've lost all hope!

When you left Coulton six years ago, I envied you so much. You had the strength and desire to better yourself—more than most people in this town, including me. I asked your mother and Granny about you from time to time, and they said you were doing well, that you graduated from college with a major in journalism and were working for the Lexington Gazette. The more I heard, the more jealous I became. When I saw you in the tavern last week, I knew I had to swallow my pride, and I purposely bumped into you. I'm sure glad I did. I guess you could say that you have become my hero and role model, and I'd like to ask for your help.

"I'll help you as much as I can. I don't know where to begin, but while I'm here for the next couple of weeks, I'll do my best," I said.

"Thank you so much!"

"It's getting late, and Mama and Granny will be worried about me," I said.

Bobbie Joe drove me home. We didn't say much, but I knew we had developed a better friendship, one that might be beneficial to both of us in the future.

When I opened the front door, I saw that Mama had placed Thanksgiving decorations throughout the house. I know she and Granny were excited about me being home for the holidays, and I was happy as well.

As I got ready for bed, I thought about my discussion with Bobbie Joe and realized the major difference between us was that his family went back generations before my grandparents settled in Coulton, and the negative stories and misconceptions about mountain people had already been handed down to thousands of families. In contrast, the Healy family had lived in the Appalachians for only four generations. By the time my family settled, a lot of those stereotypes had vanished. I didn't have the history in this town that Bobbie Joe had.

I thought about the next step for my article. Granny and Bobbie Joe had provided invaluable information that I could use. I decided I'd ask Granny if she was ready to tell me her own story.

The next morning, I woke up early. Granny was in the kitchen having breakfast. I asked if she had time to tell me about her background.

"I was waiting for you to ask!"

"Let's begin after breakfast," I said.

CHAPTER 6
GREAT-GRANNY'S STORY (PART II)

I FOUND GRANNY IN THE LIVING ROOM waiting patiently for me. She said, "Before we begin, I want to share something with you that I've kept to myself since Mama died. I was going through her belongings and found a large box with a red bow tied tightly around it. The top of the box read *Personal Do Not Open*. I decided that since she had passed, she wouldn't mind if I ignored her request. I untied the bow, opened the box, and found a number of small notebooks. Each cover had the same handwritten message—MY DIARY. I was shocked because Mama had never mentioned the diaries to me. They were numbered from one to six, and each one covered two years.

"Diary One had 1925-1927 written on it. I opened it, and the first entry was dated May 15, 1925, the day and year that Mama and Daddy got married. I read a few pages and realized the stories Mama had told me weren't the real ones. The diaries held the true story of my mama's life, and I realized that I wasn't ready to face the truth about Mama and Daddy's life. I decided not to read them, and I put them back in the box. I closed the top of the box and tied the red bow around it just like I found it."

I listened intently to Granny's revelation. She was upset, and tears rolled down her cheeks. I comforted her and asked if I could have the diaries.

"Yes, but I don't want anything to do with them," she said.

"If it's okay with you, I think we ought to postpone your story until another day," I said.

Granny agreed. I followed her to her bedroom, and she handed her mama's box to me. I hugged her and took the box to my room. Once there, I opened the box and stacked the diaries in order by date on my dresser. I picked up the first book . . . Saturday, May 15, 1925. The first line read, "I didn't know William at all, and my first night with him was frightening. I trembled uncontrollably. I didn't know what to expect. I never had a boyfriend, let alone a husband. William approached me in bed and had his way. I hated every minute and wished that I were home alone in my own bed."

I realized that Great-Granny's true story was going to be sensitive and revealing, and I felt guilty prying into her personal life. I also recognized that if I was going to author a realistic story, I had to expose both the good and bad about my family. I thought about Granny, Mama, and my siblings and their potential reaction to a newspaper article that revealed personal family secrets, but I decided that telling the true story was the only way I would attract readers. I planned to tell the story chronologically and from a cultural perspective and limit intimate details.

The next date in the diary was Wednesday, May 19. I scanned additional pages and concluded that Great-Granny did not write every day. I decided to reveal her story in sections rather than by date to trace the cultural changes she was exposed to from the first to the last diary. I wanted my readers to understand what coal town families who migrated to America in the 1920s were exposed to. I wasn't sure what categories would surface, but I thought they would reveal themselves as I read the diaries. The diary entries were written in single words, phrases, and short sentences. During my edit, I connected words and phrases to write the story in complete sentences.

Great-Granny's first diary talked about her feelings during the first two years of her life. She wrote about missing Scotland, loneliness, her first child, friends, life in Coulton, and my great-granddaddy.

After we were married, I continued to work in the fields, make meals for William, and accept his advances. I was so unhappy that I thought about running away. I didn't share my feelings with Mama or Daddy. I kept everything inside and hoped my feelings about William would change over time.

A few weeks after we were married, William told me we were going to America. I was devastated. I couldn't imagine leaving my family and everything else I loved.

After we settled in America, I was homesick every day and longed to be with my family and friends. I missed Mama, Daddy, and my brothers and sisters. I wondered what they were doing all the time. I especially missed my dog, Mickie. I longed for the days working in the potato fields and tending to the animals. It felt as if I was stranded on an island, abandoned and alone.

Once we settled in Coulton, our daily lives were the same. William worked six days a week, ten hours a day. On his day off, he slept. After Mary Lou was born, his behavior was the same. He ignored Mary Lou and me. I felt like I was raising her alone. After our second year of marriage, Timmy was born. I thought having a son would change William's neglect of Mary Lou and me. It didn't!

When I lived in Scotland, church was a constant part of my life. I observed all the religious holidays, attended church every week, and obeyed all the commandments. When I got to Coulton, I followed the same path. The church and pastor were different, but my faith in God was still the same. I noticed most of the villagers were churchgoing, honest, and respectful to one another. I was happy that they had faith in God and depended on the church to help keep that belief.

Sunday was devoted to the sermon and, afterward, fellowship in the church reception room. I was within walking distance of the church and my neighbors who attended with me. William never went to church with me or the children. He used the excuse that he was too tired. His lack of family love and participation was painful. When I confronted him, he would get angry and storm out of the house. At times, I wouldn't see him for days. Life with him was unbearable for me. I had a few friends from church who I talked to about William. Of course, Patrick and Kate were constant sounding boards. Patrick took a special interest in Mary Lou, Timmy, and me. He would show up without Kate and spend time with us. I began to enjoy his company and looked forward to his visits.

The separate housing groups continued to stay in place—poor whites on one side of the town, Black people in the hollow, and rich whites on the other side of town. Even though our houses were in various parts of town, we all got along and were friendly to one another. There were times when arguments would break out between the whites and the Black people, but they would end quickly. I think there was an unspoken connection among all of us regardless of color or money. When a celebration, town event, or holiday took place, we all got together. We celebrated holidays, anniversaries, marriages, births, and funerals together. Music and dance were important to all of us. But celebrations would often lead to drunken brawls among the men. The main troublemakers were the miners. I often thought that their behavior was a release of stress from the daily work grind. Despite their unruly behavior, they were hardworking, connected to one another, and family-loving.

A common thread among all the townspeople was their desire to live in isolation. Outsiders weren't welcome, and most families never left the mountain. Because most of the townspeople avoided contact with the outside world, there was a notion that we weren't friendly. I remember the outsiders often called us rednecks, hillbillies, and white trash. The names were used because they really didn't know us and were a bit fearful of us.

Stories about family feuds, moonshine stills, and weed-smoking, gun-carrying mountain people weren't true and created a false impression of our culture. These made-up stories were often spread outside our community by people who wanted to create a negative image so bookwriters, storytellers, and newspaper reporters could write about how ignorant and uneducated we were. A small number of people created a bad name for all of us.

I finished reading Diary One, condensing a lot of the story and omitting the more personal parts. I felt that the introductory chapter to Great-Granny's life should be written as a synopsis that exposed general information about her life.

I took a break and tried to process all I had read. I concluded that the new culture Great-Granny was exposed to was a challenge for her. I thought her first diary offered an excellent description of a culture that would either perpetuate itself from generation to generation or change over time. I recalled Bobbie Joe's story and realized that the stories Great-Granny told reinforced his own, and her feelings were similar to his negative feelings about himself.

I thought about my own life. Did I leave Coulton because I had the same feelings that Bobbie Joe had? It was a question I would come back to again and again as I authored my article.

I was anxious to begin reading the second diary and plunged into it after a quick lunch. The cover was marked Diary Two and was dated 1928-1930. Great-Granny began writing in the second diary on January 15, 1928, and she started with comments about Christmas and New Year's.

Mary Lou and Timmy enjoyed Christmas. Mary Lou was five and Timmy was three. There weren't many presents, but they enjoyed the few they had. Patrick and Kate visited with their newborn. We ate supper together and enjoyed their company. William was cheerful but drank too much. Before the evening was over, he fell asleep on the couch.

The next morning, he left for work before we got up. My only salvation was Mary Lou and Timmy. They occupied my time and kept me from think-

ing about the ill feelings I had for William. We celebrated the New Year with the townspeople. The mining company opened up their storage barn for us, and we listened to a folk music band, danced, and sang "Auld Lang Syne" at midnight.

Winter months were difficult in the mountains. Since we didn't have indoor plumbing, ice was thawed for drinking, cooking, and washing clothes. Trips to the outhouse were another story. Despite the frigid weather, we survived the winter. On weekends, we gathered for nighttime bonfires, singing, and dancing.

Overall, I had grown accustomed to my new home. William's drinking, lack of interest in the kids, and neglect of me bothered me the most. Springtime was welcomed. The trees began to leaf, flowers were in full bloom, and the warm weather was a blessing. My daily routine was the same—caring for the kids, doing chores, and hoping William would be happy.

One beautiful spring evening, I approached William and asked if he would like to talk about what was bothering him. He usually ignored me or walked away when I questioned him, but that evening, he didn't. I had high hopes that this time would be different. He told me that he wasn't a good father or husband, and he apologized. I asked him what was troubling him, and he explained his feelings and said he was disappointed with the move to America. He said that he had expected that life would be better here than in Scotland. He explained that the mining job was hard on him and that getting used to the new culture had been difficult. He felt as if he had disappointed me. I felt good that he confided in me. I asked if there was anything I could do to help. He said I had been very patient and understanding since we left Scotland, and he couldn't have asked for anything more from me. I asked him what he planned to do about the way he felt, and he said that there wasn't much he could do. He said he thought about going back to Scotland but decided that life there would be the same and the reasons we left still existed. He said we should try to make the best of it here, and he would try to change his behavior. He asked me how I felt about living in Coulton. I told him I had accepted the change. I told him I had friends and Mary Lou and Timmy kept me busy. I said my biggest concern was him—I told him that I knew he wasn't happy, his drinking didn't help, and I wanted him to spend more time with the kids and me. That would make me the happiest. He said he would do his best to change.

A few days passed before Great-Granny made another entry to the diary.

William struggled with his promise. His negative behavior toward Mary Lou, Timmy, and me was the same. He continued to pay little attention to us. There was a slight change in his behavior. I noticed that he didn't come home drunk after work, and he went straight to bed. I hoped that was a good sign.

Great-Granny continued to write about her children, her friends, and her loneliness. She wrote about her faith in God and the strength he gave her to deal with William and her longing for her family and friends in Scotland. She rarely wrote about routine responsibilities like chores or desires. Most of her entries pertained to her concerns and events that were either exciting or bothered her. I selected stories that were noteworthy and interesting to include in my article.

Toward the end of the second diary, I noticed that Great-Granny's stories were lighter and less serious. She had stopped writing about

William and her loneliness. I turned to the last page of the diary and read, *"Thank you, God, for answering my prayers."*

The entry was about Willam. She wrote that William had worked hard to change his behavior, and she was proud of him. He had stopped drinking, played with the kids, and spent more time with her. They went to all the town celebrations together and participated in all the events. She said that William hadn't had a drink in three months and had accepted Coulton better, but the mining job was still hard, working conditions hadn't improved, and money was tight.

I hadn't mentioned the diaries to Mama or told Granny I was reading them. I decided to keep things a secret for now and let them learn more about Great-Granny when they read the completed article in the newspaper. However, I continued to worry about parts of Great-Granny's diary that might be upsetting to Granny, Mama, and the rest of the family.

Thanksgiving was two days away, and I hadn't spent much time preparing with Mama and Granny. Mama mentioned we would be having Thanksgiving dinner at my brother's house. Willie was the second oldest of my siblings and had lived in Coulton his entire life. He married his high school sweetheart, and they had three children. My other two brothers and my sister were invited to Willie's also. All of the boys worked in the mines, and their wives were homemakers.

During the holidays, I thought a lot about my siblings, parents, and grandparents and their desire to live and work in Coulton. The story I was writing added a new dimension to what I knew about my family. Great-Granny's story, as told by Granny, was enlightening, but the diaries added the missing pieces. Leaving Scotland and the culture she loved and coming to America, specifically Coulton, Kentucky, presented a whole new way of life to Great-Granny. I think her loneliness and Great-Grandaddy's unhappiness might have been connected to their struggle to adapt to a strange new culture. I couldn't think of another common denominator. I thought about it over and over again and tried to come up with other reasons for her depression and Great-Grandaddy's drinking but concluded that I didn't need to look further. The diaries explained it all.

Great-Granddaddy was ten years older than Great-Granny, their marriage was arranged, they left Scotland as strangers, settled in a new culture, started a family, and struggled with bouts of loneliness and adaptation to a new way of life. Great-Granny survived the first five years because of Mary Lou, Timmy, and her faith in God. Strangely, her faith never wavered, and that faith was handed down to my generation. I hoped that Great-Granny's diaries would end happily, but I was doubtful.

I looked forward to Granny's personal story, Mama's story, Sally Mae's story, and interviews with the townspeople. I was especially interested in stories about the history of the mountain culture and how it had evolved since I was born. I finished reading Great-Granny's first two diaries and decided it was time for a break. The tavern always had live music on the Wednesday before Thanksgiving, so I decided to drive by myself just in case my friends—and of, course, Bobbie Joe—were there.

I opened the tavern door and was greeted by the loudest music imaginable and a huge crowd. I found Sally Mae and looked for Bobbie Joe but couldn't find him anywhere. I hoped he would show up later. I hung out with my friends and was having a wonderful time, but I decided to leave early so I could help Mama with the pies without an annoying hangover. While walking to the door, I checked again for Bobbie Joe, looking in every nook and cranny of the tavern. Where was he?

We gathered at Willie's farm for Thanksgiving. There were twenty-five of us in all—my two brothers, my sister, their spouses and children, Granny, Mama, and me. It made for a boisterous group! Granny's brothers and sisters had passed, and except for Mama, her children had migrated across the states for better jobs and more money than the coal mines offered. They all left Coulton after high school. Granny didn't hear from them much—an occasional letter or phone was all—and she didn't talk much about them. Perhaps she would divulge more details when she told me her story. We spent several hours with Willie and the rest of the family and looked forward to our Christmas gathering.

When I got home, I gave more thought to my sister and brothers. I was like them in some respects, but I was different when it came to leaving Coulton, going to college, and establishing a career in Lexington. My brothers were happy working in the mines, and their wives were happy caring for their children. My sister worked in a local store and was equally happy. All were hardworking, honest, and religious. They enjoyed their lifestyle and participated in the mountain culture—its music, its literature and folklore, its isolation, and its conservative approach to life. I thought about the negative names given to mountain people, and I didn't think those names applied to them. They tolerated outsiders, they weren't racists, and they weren't unwilling to accept a different point of view. They just enjoyed a simple life. In contrast, my desire to leave Coulton and explore the outside world was conceived when I was in grade school. I read a lot about different states, countries, and their cultures and vowed that I would go to college and use my education to contribute to making America better. I went to bed full of joy and anticipation for what the next day would bring.

I woke up early, fixed breakfast, and waited for Granny. She appeared in the kitchen doorway at a little after nine o'clock.

"Looks like you had a good sleep," I said.

"I was really tired after yesterday's gathering and needed an extra couple hours of sleep," she replied.

"What are your plans for the day?" I asked.

"I was expecting to start telling my story," she said.

I hadn't told her that I was reading Great-Granny's diaries because I wasn't sure she wanted to know her mother's true story. I decided to keep it a secret for a while longer. I wanted to hear Granny's story but was more interested in reading more of Great-Granny's diaries, so I told Granny we would start the next day. She shrugged and walked away, and I could tell she was disappointed.

I went to my bedroom and picked up Diary Three (1931-1933), thumbing through it to familiarize myself. The first page was dated January 15. I noticed that Great-Granny began her diaries in January and ended in December. I couldn't figure out why she had chosen the two-year period for each diary. She had just enough pages in each diary to complete the sequence. It puzzled me.

Great-Granny began the new diary with stories about Mary Lou and Timmy. She expressed how much she loved them and the enjoyment she got from being a mother. She talked about their daily routines—school, chores, and cooking. She continued to write about William's battle with alcohol and his behavior toward Mary Lou, Timmy, and her. She said that he continued to drink, but not as much. He started spending more time with them.

Most of his free time was spent trying to start a union and organizing the miners for a strike. The working conditions had not improved. Safety was a big concern along with salary and benefits. There were injuries every day and a death the first week of January. The mining company opposed the union and tried to block William's efforts. The miners became extremely angry, and the push to start a union became more real. A strike was planned, and in June it happened. The miners walked off the job and picketed the mine entrance. The mining company was furious and had armed guards brought in to end the strike and protect the scabs who were taking the jobs. On one occasion, a fight broke out between the miners and scabs. One miner was shot to death, and a number of scabs were injured. The sheriff was brought in, and a group of miners were put in jail. William was one of them. He didn't come home from work that evening, and I became concerned that he might have been killed or injured. I found out the next morning and rushed to the jail. We didn't have money for bail, so William had to spend three days in jail until his court hearing. The mining company had decided not to press charges against the miners if they would give up their plans for a union, end the strike, and return to work. They agreed even though they didn't receive better working conditions, more money, or benefits. William represented the miners and accepted the agreement. He became more bitter and angry than he was before the strike and his time in jail.

We took a short break, and I continued to read Diary Three 1931-1933.

William and I were getting along fairly well and spent many nights together talking about Scotland, our relatives, and friends we left behind. I was happy during these times and would laugh and tell stories about our small town when we was young. I loved those special evenings and thought of them often. On one occasion, just before the strike, I told William that I was pregnant and was due in August. He seemed happy with the news, but I couldn't tell if it added to the list of things that bothered him.

Two months after the strike, I went into labor. A local midwife and a neighbor helped with the delivery. I was worried about the birth because I hadn't experienced any movement for a couple of weeks. Everything was prepared for a home birth, and I was excited about number three. The midwife and the neighbor used all their experience to deliver the baby. When the baby finally arrived, I didn't hear the baby cry and knew something was wrong. My neighbor looked at me and told me the baby was stillborn. I cried uncontrollably and asked for William, but he didn't come. I recovered from the loss but kept the memory. I was deeply upset with William and never forgave him for not being with me.

The remaining months of 1931 were spent on daily routines, church, family time, town celebrations, and holidays. I thought about the loss of our son Charles and my loneliness, and I hoped the new year would be more positive.

I put the diary on the table next to my bedroom window and thought about the difficult year Great-Granny had. The loss of a child was the worst thing she had to endure, but the strike, a miner's death, and William's time in jail also bothered her immensely. I concluded that my great-granny was quite resilient.

I took a break to have lunch with Mama and Granny.

"Are we still on for tomorrow?" Granny asked.

"Yes, let's meet in the living room at nine," I said.

"How are things going with the article?" asked Mama.

"Good," I said. "Granny finished telling me about Great-Granny, and we're going to start her story tomorrow." I didn't mention Great-Granny's diaries.

I left the kitchen and returned to my room, anxious to read what happened in 1933. Before reading it, I decided to call Ben and tell him about my progress. He answered my call immediately.

"How's it going, Mo?" he asked.

"I've been working on the project for almost two weeks and would like to email the first couple of chapters," I replied.

"That's great. I look forward to reading them."

"I thought Great-Granny's story was finished, but to my surprise, Granny found a box filled with her mother's diaries. I'm reading them now and discovering that she had a whole different life that Granny knew nothing about. It will add a lot to the story," I said.

"Sounds good. I'll look for your email," said Ben.

When I got off the phone, I reviewed and edited the article, deleting my personal information. I didn't think that the paper's readers would care about my relationship with Bobbie Joe or my family's Thanksgiving. I completed the first draft and sent it to Ben.

Then, I returned to the diaries. Great-Granny's next entry was on January 3, 1933. She began with a description of the harsh winter they were experiencing.

School had been closed for a week, and Mary Lou and Timmy were driving me crazy. The mine was closed, so William was home too. We made the best of it . . . playing in the snow, building a snowman, and having a snowball war. I was surprised that William spent so much time with us. I was happy! The biggest concern for all the townspeople was the Great Depression. It began in 1929, and its ill effects were felt by all the townspeople. The mining company tried to keep the miners working but eventually offered daytime work only.

By 1933, the Depression worsened. Money was scarce and food was often limited. Most depended on their gardens and hunting for food. Coulton's families banded together and helped one another through the tragedy. They brought food to the church food bank where a distribution center was set up. William and I had a garden since coming to Coulton and were able to contribute to the food distribution center during the growing season. I put up vegetables and fruit, and William hunted for small and large game. We struggled at times but were able to survive with our own food and the help of the food bank.

During the ten years that the Depression lasted, the Coulton culture of sharing strengthened. Poor whites, Black people, and the rich were all faced with the same hardships and were dependent on one another. I benefited from the Depression. I felt less lonely and more connected to my family, friends, and church. Despite the trauma that the Depression brought, we lived through it, and in some respects, it helped me.

The Depression was the major event that Great-Granny wrote about in 1933. She also told stories about Mary Lou and Timmy. Patrick and Kate were mentioned a few times.

They were constant visitors and helped when they could. Patrick continued his solo visits. He would often show up when William wasn't home. I liked his company and became closer to him, often confiding my feelings about William.

Great-Granny concluded the diary in December of 1933 with a description of a bleak Christmas and the hope that the new year would be better. I picked up Diary 4 (1934-36) and began reading. The first entry was dated January 7, 1934.

The new year began with the same strife and peril. Food was more scarce due to the harsh winter. We used most of the canned goods. I had stored food and became less dependent on the church food bank. The mine had reopened shifts, and William was back to work full time. The supply of coal that was used in northern factories had been used up, so there was a call for more coal. The frigid winter had increased the demand, and states across the country were in short supply. William was happy, and so was I. The weather improved, and the kids were back in school full time, which made my days long. I kept busy with quilting and knitting and was fortunate to sell a few pieces in the company store. I used the money to help with buying what little food the store had.

The warmth of spring brought some relief. I planted vegetables and pruned the fruit trees. I made every effort to ensure that we would have food for the winter. Summer came quickly, and we enjoyed the fresh produce. Despite the Depression, the villagers celebrated July 4th with the customary bang. Mary Lou and Timmy grew like wildflowers—Mary Lou was nine and Timmy was seven. Had Charles lived, he would have been three years old. I wanted to have another child but realized that the tough times would make it even more difficult for us . . . another mouth to feed. I recognized the hardship it would present but felt another child would be good for Mary Lou, Timmy, and me. I wasn't sure William would agree. I didn't discuss my desire with William but planned to have a child despite his anticipated opposition.

Near the end of summer, I realized I was pregnant, and the baby was due in November. I approached William and told him. He shrugged his shoulders in anger and walked out of the house. I prayed that the baby would be a boy and healthy, not only to replace Charles but to encourage William to take more interest in the children.

We moved through the rest of the year without any hardships. William's anger had slowed, the kids enjoyed school, and I did my daily routine. Kevin was born on November 19, 1934, and the delivery went smoothly. My biggest surprise was William's reaction to his new son. He was with me during the delivery and smiled at me after the birth. He held Kevin in his arms the day he was born. I was happy that he arrived healthy and was overjoyed that William had taken to him. We celebrated Thanksgiving and Christmas joyfully and ended the year with our newborn son and looking forward to a brighter future.

The new year (1935) came in like a lion. I hoped it would leave like a lamb. The Depression continued, the weather was harsh, food was again scarce, and money was nonexistent. I made a few dollars selling quilts, scarves, and hats at the company store. William's hours at the mine had been cut again, so he brought home less money than the previous year. The villagers continued to help us and support one another. I was proud of the good relationship I had with them. I felt that I had become more accepting of Coulton and the mountain culture.

CHAPTER 7
GRANNY'S STORY

I HAD FINISHED READING FOUR OF Great-Granny's diaries—1925-1927, 1928-1930, 1931-1933, and 1934-1936. The most notable entries were stories about the Depression that began in 1929. Its effects around the world were devastating, and Coulton was no exception. I was glued to the diaries and wanted to continue reading through the night, but I knew Granny would be anxious to tell her story in the morning, so I went to bed. The next morning, I found Granny in the living room, already seated and ready to begin.

Before Daddy died, Mama and Daddy had three more children. Charles was born in 1931, Kevin in 1935, and Peter in 1938. I was born after Daddy died. Mama talked a lot about Charles's death. It was one of the saddest times of her life. She said Daddy continued to work as hard as he could to make ends meet, but they were still feeling the effects of the Depression.

Food was the biggest problem. Since they were isolated in the mountains, food wasn't always available from week to week. Most depended on their vegetable gardens and small game to survive. The church continued its food bank but was short on what they had. Despite the tough times, special occasions were still celebrated, and the townspeople did their best they could to survive.

Most of Mama's time was spent caring for the children. In 1935, Kevin was born. He was born with a bad cold and almost died. Mama nursed Kevin from day one and eventually he got better. Mary Lou was in third grade and Timmy in first grade. Both enjoyed school, and Mama was happy she could spend more time taking care of Kevin. Mama often said that Daddy wasn't much help. He spent little time with Mary Lou and my brothers. He was either working, sleeping, or drunk. Mama said that having a lot of children was a way of life for mountain people. They provided joy and kept the culture alive.

When she wasn't tending to her children, Mama did house chores, worked in the garden, spent time at church, and enjoyed the company of friends. She thought a lot about Scotland but wasn't as lonely as when she first came to America. She accepted that she would never see her mama, daddy, or brothers and sisters again. She said her childhood memories would always have a special place in her heart.

In 1938, Mama had her fifth child. He was named Peter. She realized having so many children would be hard on her and Daddy, but in the long run, they made her happy and less lonely. Having the fifth child was more than Daddy could manage. He was drunk most of the time and useless to her.

Finally, in 1939, the Depression ended, and the future looked brighter. The mine was in full production, and William brought home enough money to buy more and better food that came to the company store. The townspeople were happier, and times felt good. Mama said just when she thought times had changed for the better, Daddy's lung disease got worse. He stopped working and was bedridden. She cared for him as best she could, but he died on January 2, 1940. Mama was left with four children and didn't know what to do. The mining company had provided life insurance, and because Mary Lou was working for them, they were able to keep the house.

The entire town grieved Daddy's death. Over the years he had done so much for the miners and their families. Mama said Patrick and Kate were a tremendous comfort. She was very lonely, and their company was extremely helpful. Patrick would often visit without Kate, and they struck up a special relationship. She would often break down in tears, and Patrick would hold her tightly in his arms. One night, she was so sad and lonely that his comfort turned to passion. That night their relationship turned into more than friendship.

Because Mama lost Daddy's income, she got a job at the company store. Timmy and Kevin were in school while she worked, and a neighbor watched Peter. Within a couple of months, Mama realized she was pregnant. She said she was devastated. Daddy was gone, and she had no one to lean on and felt her whole life was broken. Having a child the same year her husband died was difficult to explain. She said she decided to have the baby and accept the consequences ahead of her. She turned to God and the church. The pastor guided her through the pregnancy, and she continued to work at the store. Her sixth child was born in November. She was healthy, and she named her Lisa Marie.

I couldn't believe what Granny had just told me. My mind drew a blank. Granny's birth after her daddy had died was troubling. Was Granny's father Patrick? If so, Great-Granny had said nothing to her about the possibility. Of course, she was too young to understand what was going on. I had a tough time accepting what I had just read. I wondered if Mama knew about the possibility that Patrick was Granny's father.

I was so shaken by the revelation that I cried myself to sleep. I woke up in the middle of the night, fully dressed, and remembered Granny telling me about being born the same year her daddy died. I couldn't comprehend what Great-Granny had gone through. I was sure that Granny didn't know the whole story. I went back to sleep, hoping it was just a dream.

When I woke up the next morning, I thought about what to do. Should I ask Mama if she knew that Patrick might be Granny's father? Should I confront Granny? But I did nothing.

I was confused and upset and had to talk to someone, so I called Sally. We met in the park next to Coulton Creek.

Sally Mae took one look at my face and saw how upset I was. "What's with the gloomy face?" she asked.

I broke down in tears and told her what I had found out.

"What are you going to do?" she asked.

"So far, nothing. I'm not sure what to do," I replied.

"Well, maybe it's best that you keep quiet to your granny and try to find out if your mother knows about it," she said.

I agreed but dreaded the outcome.

I thought about skipping Book Five and starting with Book Six but knew that would mean missing two years of Great-Granny's story. So, I went home, picked up Book Five, and began reading where I had left off.

Great-Granny continued her story about the Depression and the hardships it presented for Coulton and her family.

The effects of the Depression still lingered in 1940. Little by little, more food became available. The mine was in full production, and a small amount of relief was felt. Just prior to the new year, William fell sick. The lung disease had taken hold, and he stopped working. His illness didn't last long, and he died in January. He knew he had lung disease but still worked every day to support our family. His loss affected me hard and was felt by the whole community. I struggled with his loss through the year and was guilt-ridden about the baby's birth.

The year ended, and with it the Depression, and good times were shared by all despite my trials. The coal business was booming, food was plentiful, and most of the townspeople had smiles on their faces. The mining company had opened a vein in Coulton, and all the miners and their families were happy because they no longer had to take the six-mile train to Harlin. I continued to work in the company store and Mary Lou in the new office next to the mine. Timmy and Kevin were in school, and Peter and Lisa Marie were cared for by a neighbor. I enjoyed being a part of the community and the culture that had developed. We went to all the town celebrations and events. God and fellowship with the church parishioners were a big part of my life.

By 1943, I had grown used to living without William. The children took up most of my time. Overall, I was reasonably happy. Patrick and Kate would visit occasionally, and we would talk about Scotland, William, and our children. On separate occasions, Patrick would show up by himself. We never talked about the evening we spent together before William died. There was the unspoken possibility that our relationship that evening was more than friendship. Patrick would spend time with all the children but gave special attention to Lisa Marie.

I finished reading the last page of the final diary, Book Six (1940-1942). The last entry ended with the words "THE END."

I thought about either calling Ben to give him an update on my progress or contacting Bobbie Joe to see how he was doing. I went with updating Ben.

He answered his phone immediately. "How's it going?" he asked.

"The interview with Granny is on target. She has remarkable recall. Her mother began telling her stories about her life when she was six years old and continued until she was eleven. The content is mostly about raising her children, day-to-day life with friends and the church, and the difficulties she had with her husband, William. Granny gave detailed information about the Depression and the effects of her father's death. In between interviews, I read Great-Granny's diaries that Granny found after her death. Her stories are quite revealing and forthcoming. Great-Granny revealed that she and William's friend had a relationship after he died. The possibility that Granny's father is Patrick is likely. I haven't mentioned it to Granny or my mother. I want to see if they know about the possibility.

"Great-Granny's diaries and Granny's stories suggest that the townspeople had a strong bond and developed a unique culture exclusive to Appalachia. They socialized with each other, shared hardships, and supported one another. Although there were three distinct class structures—poor whites, Black people, and the rich—they all got along like one big happy family. They were proud of the heritage that had been handed down for generations. Despite outsider negativity, they held fast to their Baptist faith, isolated lifestyle, and culture."

Ben didn't interrupt me during my story capsulation but finally said, "Wow, you've certainly learned a lot about your hometown and family. You have the beginnings of a unique story that our readers will love. Keep up the magnificent work and let me know how you're doing from time to time. I appreciate all you've done so far. Keep up the good work."

After I finished talking to Ben, I looked for Granny. I hadn't talked with her about continuing her story, but I knew she wanted to tell me about her school life. I found her in the kitchen and asked if she wanted to talk. We agreed to meet the next day at nine in the living room.

I went to my bedroom and called Bobbie Joe. He didn't answer but called back ten minutes later. I waited for the fifth ring to answer because I didn't want him to think I was just sitting there waiting for him to call.

"How's it going," I asked.

"All well here," he replied.

"I was hoping we could get together again before Christmas or before I leave," I said.

"I'd love to," he responded.

"Would you like to meet at the tavern this Saturday?" I asked.

"Nine o'clock?"

"Sounds good, see you then," I replied. I wanted to see how he was doing after our lengthy discussion about his family's history and also get more input on his feelings about Coulton and his desire to do more with his life.

I laid down on my bed and fell asleep, but I didn't sleep well. I kept thinking about Great-Granny's last diary. There were so many unanswered questions that bothered me. My update with Ben had gone well, but I still questioned whether my story would contribute to selling more papers. If nothing else, I had learned a lot about my family and the mountain culture. I thought about Bobbie Joe and if there was any future with him.

"Are you ready?" I asked.

"Whenever you are," she said.

You know I was born the same year that Daddy died. I was the last of Mama's children. There were five before me, and Mama often said I was the runt of the litter. Mary Lou was the oldest, and she cared for me most of the time while Mama was working at the company store and trying to make ends meet. I can't say that I remember much before I was five, but

I do remember Mama telling me the story about a party in a barn where Daddy got sick, and Mama kicked him while he was lying on the dirt floor. She said she was so upset that she grabbed Mary Lou and Timmy and took them home without Daddy. I've always wondered why that story stayed with me. Maybe it's because I've heard so many negative stories about Daddy that happened because he was a drunk.

Granny paused for a minute and stared out the window.

"Are you okay?" I asked.

"I'm fine, but that memory still haunts me," she said. And then she continued.

Mama told me other stories about the Depression and how food was scarce, and she and Daddy had to grow their own food and hunt for meat. She said the church had a food bank that they depended on. The Depression ended the year before Daddy died, and Mama said life was better till Daddy got sick. The mining company started putting out a lot of coal, and the miners were happy. They had more money in their pockets than they'd had for a long while.

Mama said there was a world war going on and many of the young boys from Coulton were fighting in it. I didn't know much about the war, and it really didn't affect me. The opposite was true of other families. You know, many of those boys didn't come home.

The mine was in full operation supplying coal to the big northern cities where wartime production was in full swing. Jobs outside of Appalachia became plentiful, and a number of families left for the promise of a better life. All of Coulton did their best to make a strong contribution to winning the war.

In 1945, the war ended, and we all celebrated. Local, state, and federal government programs were started that benefited Coulton. New businesses, jobs, and modernization came to the mountains. Road and bridge construction offered work for all with good pay and benefits. We finally got electricity, plumbing, and heat. Many felt rich!

Granny paused and glanced at me before beginning her grade school stories.

I started first grade in a one-room schoolhouse. There was no heat, indoor plumbing, or electricity. We froze in the winter and sweated during the hot months. All the kids from first to eighth grade were in one classroom with one teacher. I thought she was a magician to be able to teach twenty kids of all ages who were learning different stuff. I liked school a lot and had lots of friends. We played outdoor games all year 'round. Even during the winter, we would find something to do.

Mary Lou had finished eighth grade and started working as a bookkeeper for the mining company. She was only thirteen and worked ten hours a day. There were no child labor laws, so the mining company took advantage of her. Mama said Mary Lou never complained because she knew she was helping to put food on the table. My three brothers and I went to school every day from September to June. Mama was a stickler about school and wanted us to get as much schooling as possible.

Mama started telling me some of her stories when I was six years old and stopped when Mary Lou died in 1955. She was only thirty, and I was eleven. Mary Lou's death was a shock and felt deeply by her friends and family. I was especially affected because she was my best friend. I stopped seeing my school friends and hardly talked to Mama and my brothers. I was lonely without her and longed for a friend to replace her.

During my early school years, I had lots of friends at school and at home. Many of them were miner's children, but I also played with Black kids and rich kids . . . that's what we called them. I learned that the mine families were called poor whites.

I remember an incident when one of the rich kids was picking on a smaller Black friend. I picked up a stick and went after her. She ran away as fast as she could. Later, she became one of my best friends. She lived in Coulton her whole life and passed a couple of years ago. I still have fond memories of her.

I was a good student and enjoyed math the most. I often thought about being a teacher. As you know, that never happened for obvious reasons.

In 1945, WWII ended. I was five years old. As I said, I knew nothing about the war—only that the whole town was happy. Some of the Coulton boys were killed, some came home injured, and the lucky ones were greeted with a big celebration. None of the boys was in the war because they were too young when it started. The boys who returned home uninjured were given their mine jobs back. Some decided to leave Coulton for better jobs and a better life.

When the war ended, a government program called the New Deal was started by President Franklin Delano Roosevelt, and a lot of new jobs started. He created jobs to build roads and bridges. A program called the TVA started to dam rivers for electricity. There was many new programs. One that was really important to Coulton was forest and water protection. Over the years, mining had caused the mountains to erode and pollute the streams.

Another very popular program for workers started. It was called Social Security. The miners were happy because it put more money in their paychecks and built up savings for retirement. Those who left Coulton for a better life were able to take advantage of the new programs.

The period was the start of a new time for the industrialization and modernization of America. Car and truck repair shops, five-and-dime stores, gas stations, and small businesses sprung up everywhere. Electricity and indoor plumbing became the norm. Coulton had become a modern town.

Mama and Mary Lou continued to work for the mining company—Mama in the company store and Mary Lou in the office next to the mine. The news about the new programs really didn't affect me at all. I continued to enjoy my family and friends.

Granny decided to take a break, and it gave me time to mentally review Granny's story. She said she continued to have long talks with her mother until she was fifteen. Her mother would often relive the past. She'd talk about Granddaddy, the children, and her life in Coulton. She continued to work at the store, visit her friends, and attend church services. She talked about Patrick's death occasionally but never mentioned anything about an intimate relationship. She missed her cousin Kate and told stories about growing up together in Scotland.

When Granny returned to the living room, she continued her story.

I was happy living in Coulton. I had so many friends and had a carefree life. Mary Lou was my best friend, and we confided in each other. She never had a boyfriend and spent most of her time at work, helping Mama, and playing with me. She had a couple of girlfriends but didn't spend much time with them. Mama always worried because she seemed different from most girls her age. I think she missed the most important years of her life because she had to grow up early because of Daddy's death and get a job to help out.

I would think about Daddy once and for a while, but I never missed him because I never knew him. Patrick was always there and, in some respects, became my father.

There isn't really much to say about the years before I reached my teens. I thought my life was good. Mama was happy, and we got along well. Mary Lou worked hard but always found time for me. Timmy, Kevin, and Peter were normal older brothers. They teased me all the time and used me as a guinea pig. I remember one time when they made a wooden slide off the outhouse roof and told me I could be the first to use it. I climbed a ladder and got to the roof, sat down, and began to slide. Within seconds, I realized I had made a bad decision. My behind was filled with slivers, and I was in terrible pain. My brothers laughed all the way back to the house. Mama wasn't happy and made all three clean the outhouse, wash windows, and apologize. The boys always tried to play tricks on me, but I never fell for them again. Despite their childhood pranks, I loved them dearly.

Coulton had developed into a bigger and lively town. New stores opened, including a soda and candy store. It was my favorite, and when I earned money, which wasn't often, that's where you would find me on a Saturday morning. A movie theater opened that showed movies on the weekends. I only went a couple of times, but I got to know the names of famous actors like Natalie Wood and Maureen O'Hara. The movie I liked the best was Miracle on 34th Street.

Granny paused and looked at me. "Your mother named you after her," she said. Seconds later, she continued her story.

The town celebrations continued. It seemed as if all of Coulton was there. Music, dancing, and drinking remained the most popular activities. I loved playing with my friends and looked forward to every holiday party.

A few families had left for better jobs and more money, but most stayed because they liked the culture that had developed over the years. Most accepted our way of life. Sometimes outsiders would occasionally visit Coulton. They were usually reporters looking to question our lifestyle and how we survived living in poverty. Mama said they just wanted to help us get a better life. I think they went back to the big cities and wrote stories describing us as white hillbilly trash who were an embarrassment to the country. I think they never talked about the success of our boys who fought in the war, the importance of the coal mines, and the families that left Coulton to make America great.

Granny stopped and said, "There are so many more stories I could tell you about Mama, Mary Lou, and my brothers that would add pages to your article, but most wouldn't be interesting. The years from when I was eleven to thirteen passed by quickly. My teen years were more exciting and more interesting."

In 1953, I turned thirteen. The teen years were a milestone for me. I became a "woman" that spring. My whole personality seemed to change. I went from bobby socks to stockings overnight. I started to take an interest in boys, and my first crush was in seventh grade.

Perry was a miner's son who lived next door. We would often talk about our futures. His family left Coulton after eighth grade and moved to Columbus, Ohio. Perry's parents wanted him to go to high school and college. They didn't want him to be a miner like his daddy or marry a miner's daughter. Mama heard that he went to college and became a highly successful lawyer.

When I finished eighth grade, I was fourteen years old. My only option was to get a job with the mining company. Mary Lou was still working in the office and Mama in the company store. I didn't much care for office work, so I got a job with Mama. I had already been working with her for a year and didn't know what else I could do. I thought about leaving Coulton—but where would I go?

The day that Mary Lou died changed my whole life. Mama and I had just finished our work at the store and started our walk home. We were halfway there when we heard an explosion coming from the mine. The sound was deafening, and black smoke filled the air. We ran toward the mine and saw flames and smoke coming from what was left of the building where Mary Lou worked. We were beside ourselves and fell to the ground, praying that she had gotten out in time. A fireman approached us and said there were no survivors. We walked home in tears and gave my brothers the tragic news. For days, I trembled when I thought about Mary Lou. There was a church funeral with a small gathering, and Mary Lou was laid to rest next to Daddy under the old elm tree in the town cemetery.

Weeks and months passed, and I was lonelier than ever until I met your granddaddy, Harry. I was sixteen, and he was eighteen. He worked in the mine and would stop by the store after I finished work, and we would talk about everything. I guess you could say I was in love with him. We weren't married when I got pregnant with Max, but we got married before he was born on May 6, 1955. We started our lives with a surprise baby and a mining company rental.

All my dreams about leaving Coulton and continuing my schooling were gone. Harry was a good man and treated me with respect and concern. Whether we were in love was questionable. Maybe he replaced Mary Lou.

I adjusted to my new life and gave Max all my love. Harry was happy with our lives. We participated in all the town celebrations and functions and were avid churchgoers who dedicated our lives to God.

Around 1956, around fifty miners left Coulton for the big cities and better jobs. Most miners were poor and thought leaving was for the best, but many came back when they realized their new lifestyle was not what they had hoped. Most had never left Coulton and the security of the mountain culture. When they got to the big northern cities, they had to adjust to a new culture. They weren't always accepted. People thought they were backward and uneducated, and they questioned their way of life. The mountain language and accent were new to the city folk. The miners' isolated lives hadn't prepared them for the cultural change, and many had a tough time.

Harry and I decided not to leave Coulton. He thought what was good for his daddy was good for him, and I agreed. I was young and attached to my siblings and the routine of mountain life. We had our rough patches over the years but always thought we made the right decision to not leave Coulton. That decision wasn't accepted by your brothers when they got older. Angela was our second child, and she was an angel. We enjoyed watching her grow with leaps and bounds. When she got older, she left Coulton unexpectedly.

Harry complained about working in the mine but knew there was no other option. His daily routine never changed—work, eat, and sleep. There wasn't much entertainment in Coulton. We thought about going to Lexington but never did. When the black and white TVs came out, we saved enough money to buy one. There weren't as many programs to watch like today. But just the same, we enjoyed lots of shows and watched them faithfully.

Coulton had a small movie house that showed films on the weekends. We went once and a while but pretty much stayed at home. Mama was fifty-five years old at this time, and we visited her weekly. She caught us up on all the local gossip.

I thought about Mary Lou all the time and wished she was alive to see Angela. Mary Lou never married, and there had always been suspicion that she was gay. She dated a couple of boys in high school and that was about it. The idea that she liked girls was confirmed when she moved in with her best friend when she was twenty-five. To be gay in Coulton was a religious disgrace. She was shunned by the townspeople, especially those who were strict Baptists. There was an attempt by the pastor to have her reborn, but she never accepted the church invitation. She was happy with her job and partner. I never questioned her choices—I was just pleased because she was happy. While she was alive, we spoke all the time about everything.

Timmy, Kevin, and Peter worked in the mine. They were all married with a flock of kids. I never understood how they could support their families with the money they made at the mine. There was talk in town they were strip-mining on the side to make extra money. There was also a rumor that they were connected with the Black people and making moonshine and growing weed. I suspected all three were true.

Max had turned three, and we decided to have another child. In 1960, Angela was born. She was a delight, and Harry doted on her constantly and took her everywhere with him. I often thought he was preparing her to work in the mine when she was two years old. We weren't good churchgoers after Mary Lou died because of the way the church treated her, but at Mama's insistence, Max and Angela were baptized. The celebration was attended by most of the townspeople. There was tons of mountain food, music, dancing, and 'shine. To keep busy, I followed in Mama's footsteps and quilted and crocheted. I made a little extra money to help with the bills.

In 1960, President Kennedy was elected. He was extremely popular, and most people in Coulton liked him even though he was Catholic. He had a beautiful wife and little children that made him liked by American families. He was on the side of the poor and started programs to help. He was especially concerned with the poor whites and Black people of Appalachia. JFK's presidency lasted only four years. He was assassinated in 1964.

Gregory was born the year before JFK died. He was as healthy and as happy as could be. We were happy to have him despite our never-ending poverty.

President Kennedy's vice president, LBJ, became president. He passed the Civil Rights Act and started the War on Poverty program to deal with discrimination and help the poor.

As the years passed, I came to realize that poor white Appalachians were no different from Black people. Both groups were often born in poverty and discriminated against, and they struggled for most of their lives. I didn't know much about what was happening on the other side of the mountain and depended on Harry to keep me up to date. The population in Coulton was approximately six hundred. The poor white group numbered around four hundred, and the Black people and rich whites was about one hundred each. There was a clear difference between the poor whites, Black people, and the rich. Most poor whites and Black people had no more than an eighth-grade education and worked in the mine or farmed. The rich were high school educated, managed the mine, owned the shops, and owned the land. Many thought the Civil Rights Act and the War on Poverty Program would create more educational opportunities and decrease poverty for poor whites and Black people. There were a couple of benefits from the programs. A new elementary school was built in Harlan, and a high school was built in the county and more teachers were hired. The kids from Coulton no longer walked to school and were bused to the new schools in large yellow buses every day. Rather than going to separate schools, the whites, Black people, and rich all went to the same schools together. The biggest change was that all the children—poor or rich—could go to high school. Coulton had grown into a community where whites, Black people, and the rich got along with little discrimination. Of course, all three groups knew their place.

Families that left Coulton for better education and jobs returned with stories that the Civil Rights Act wasn't successful and the War on Poverty had failed. I remember finishing my day at the company store and walking by the Greyhound station. Four young people with suitcases got off a bus. I was surprised and wondered who they were and why they were in Coulton, so I walked toward them and introduced myself. They said they were college students from the UK and were volunteers for a program called VISTA. I had never heard of it and asked what it meant. One of the two girls said the letters stood for Volunteers in Service to America. I asked what kind of service they were going to give, and one of the boys said that there was a movement in America to help the poor in Appalachia. When I asked how it would help us, he said it would improve education, strengthen health services, decrease unemployment, and eliminate the negative perception outsiders have about people from Appalachia. I wanted to know how they were going to do that, and they told me they were going to learn more about us and tell us more about them. Then they would organize groups to help reduce poverty. I wasn't sure if what they said was even possible. The problems in Coulton had existed for so long, and there had already been programs that had failed. I walked them to Betty Jane's boarding house where they would be staying, and then went home.

When Harry came home from the mine, I told him the whole story. He said he had heard about VISTA but wasn't sure what it was all about. He said from what he knew, the program was started by President Kennedy and President Johnson. There were thousands of college student volunteers who had been trained to help improve human services and strengthen community development. I told Harry that I had met four VISTA volunteers in town and asked them why they were in Coulton. They explained what they were going to do, and I asked how they knew what we needed. My friend Joe said they wanted to help organize us to fight strip-mining because it was ruining the land, streams, farming, and logging. He said that they wanted to help us with our welfare rights, health care, and other town problems. I told Harry that it all sounded good to me, but they sure better learn who we are and why we've chosen our way of life.

The four volunteers arranged a meeting at the church to introduce themselves and explain why they were in Coulton. At the meeting, lots of people asked questions and told them some things about us. I remember my friend Marie told them we had a heritage of working-class values and solidarity. We liked our isolation and were tired of being taken advantage of by politicians, the mine owners, and landowners who didn't pay their fair share of taxes. We lived in poverty because of the mining companies' self-interest and greed and government neglect. The meeting ended, and Harry and I talked more about it when we got home. We agreed that health care, welfare rights, housing, and education were important issues that we were all concerned about. Harry said that the poor needed to take control of their lives and do something about government programs that didn't work, politicians who were self-serving, and the mining company control. He said something needed to be done about unemployment and the enormous difference between the haves and the have-nots.

The VISTA volunteers started their work and organized local and regional politicians, government agencies, and villagers to eliminate strip-mining and address mine safety, unemployment, education, and human and social services. Over time, some gains were made—until the Vietnam War needed money and the VISTA program money was given to the war effort. There were protests about the war across America. President Nixon cut the poverty money to support the war and reduce welfare costs and growing transfer payments. There was a significant decline in community action groups who worked hard to help Coulton. Those who benefited from the government payments voiced their opposition to the Medicaid and Medicare cuts. Doctors, druggists, grocers, and bankers all lost money when government programs were cut.

When the money for the VISTA program was lost, the Coulton volunteers left to pursue their careers and never returned. Since I never left Coulton, I wasn't really sure what was happening on the other side of the mountain. I was happy about the new schools and better educational opportunities and hoped that our children would get a better education than Harry and me, but kids being bused bothered me.

As time passed, the relationship among the poor whites, Black people, and the rich stayed the same. I think we all got along because of money—all of us lived according to our means. The poor whites kept the mine open, the Black people farmed, and the rich benefited by owning the land and businesses and making money off the poor.

I tried to absorb all that Granny had said, but it was overwhelming. She knew a lot about real life on both sides of the mountain. I had enough notes and recordings to keep me busy for days, so I thanked Granny and gave her a big hug.

"How about we take a break for a couple of days?" I said.

I had been interviewing Granny and reading the diaries for almost two weeks and hoped I could put all the information into an interesting and readable written form. The toughest part of my assignment was writing the story in the language in which it was told.

I hadn't forgotten my Saturday night date with Bobbie Joe. I wondered how he was doing and if he had made any decisions about his future. As I worked on the article over the next couple of days, I became excited about meeting up with him.

I drove to the tavern and arrived just before nine. Bobbie Joe was sitting in a booth next to the bar. He looked at me and gave me a big smile.

"What are you so happy about?" I asked.

"Would you like a drink?" he asked, ignoring my question. I nodded, and he was off to the bar.

He knew I liked gin, so a gin and tonic it was. He sat down, looked me straight in the eyes, and said, "I've made a huge decision that might change my whole life."

"What's that?" I asked.

"I'm going to college."

I was surprised and wanted to know more. "Please explain," I said.

Bobbie Joe told me he had applied to UK for the spring semester. He was taking a couple of required courses and had applied to the mechanical engineering school for fall enrollment. I looked at him, then reached over and gave him a big hug.

"Where will you live? Will you get a job? Are you scared? Will you have time to see me?"

After being bombarded with all my questions, he answered only one. "Yes, I will have time to see you."

"Wow, that's amazing! I'm so happy for you!" I said.

We hung out in the booth and talked for a couple of hours. I volunteered to help him find an apartment and show him around Lexington. We walked to our cars together, kissed, and then I headed home.

When I walked into the kitchen, Mama was sitting at the table. It was after midnight, and Mama never stayed up past eleven. She looked worried.

"Is everything okay?" I asked.

"Granny has had a fever all day, and I'm really concerned about her," she said.

"Should we take her to the hospital in Lexington?"

"I think we might have to if her fever doesn't break by morning."

I followed Mama upstairs, and we peeked in on Granny. She was sound asleep.

The next morning, Mama and I woke Granny and checked her temperature. It was 101.4. We bundled her up and headed to Mt. Hill Hospital. We arrived within an hour and entered through the emergency door. After checking Granny in, we waited to be called to her room. We found her awake but listless. She perked up a bit when she saw us, but she wasn't the Granny I had been interviewing the past couple of weeks. The doctor told us she had COVID. Mama and Granny had been very careful not to be exposed during the pandemic and were successful in not catching the disease. On the other hand, I had COVID twice and had just received the all-clear before I came home. My mind reeled.

Did Granny catch the disease from me?

We talked to her doctor, and she advised us that Granny should stay in the hospital for a couple of days to be certain the COVID medicine helped and her respiration was okay.

Mama looked at Granny and said, "Take care. We will see you later." Fortunately, I had an apartment in Lexington, and it was minutes away from the hospital.

The next afternoon, we visited Granny, and the doctor said her fever had broken, the medicine was working, and her lungs were clear. We were relieved and looked forward to taking her home.

I gave Ben a call to tell him about Granny and said I would stop and see him tomorrow. Granny was my big concern right now, not because I wanted her to finish her story but because I wanted her to get better.

The next day, I dropped Mama off at the hospital and drove to the *Gazette*. Ben was in his office and invited me in. I gave him an update, and he seemed pleased. I highlighted the discovery of Great-Granny's diary and told Ben I was pursuing the possibility that Granny's father was a longtime friend of her daddy's. I also gave him a lot of detail about the mountain culture and how it had evolved from the Scottish settlement in 1820 to the present.

He was especially interested in the culture, so I explained that the mountain people were clannish, preferred isolation to large cities, and bonded through religion, folk music, and language. I also told him more about the class structure and the strong cohesiveness among the poor whites, Black people, and rich despite their economic disparity. I mentioned that the mountain people were tired of being perceived as hillbillies, rednecks, and white trash by outsiders, and my story was going to show the truth about them and debunk the misconceptions outsiders had of them. When my article was finished, I believed that the attitudes and opinions of outsiders would change, and the mountain people would see a hopeful future and a path toward eliminating poverty.

Ben listened intently, then sat back in his chair. "It's hard to believe you've learned so much in such a short time. I'm impressed and believe you are on your way to writing and telling a timely and much-needed story. Continue your pursuit. I look forward to our next update."

I thanked him and left to go to the hospital to check on Granny.

When I got there, Mama told me Granny was much better, and we could take her home the next day. The doctor said we would need to keep an eye on her for a few days. I was relieved but couldn't shake the possibility that Granny had caught COVID from me. We picked Granny up early the next day and headed for home.

Back at the house, I settled in and thought about Bobbie Joe's decision to pursue his dreams. I vowed to help him as much as I could. But my greatest concern was still Granny. I prayed that night that she would get better. I planned to work on my story for the next couple of days and hoped she would be able to continue.

Two days had passed, and I had been checking on Granny religiously. On the third day, I asked if she was up to talking to me again about her story. She looked at me and said, "I was wondering when you would ask." Granny was back!

I reminded Granny that we had left off in the midsixties after JFK had been assassinated and LBJ took over as president. Both had been deeply concerned about poverty, education, and discrimination. The Civil Rights Act had been passed, and the War on Poverty program was started. I asked Granny what she knew about the Vietnam War.

I know that the US sent soldiers in 1965, a year before Ralph was born. There were lots of boys from Coulton who volunteered, just like in WWII and the Korean War. Some made it home, and some didn't. The loss was felt by the whole town, and a monument was put up in the square to honor the veterans from all wars. Each year on Memorial Day, veterans speak about their patriotism and the need to end all wars. Of course, no one listens because we keep having them.

The Vietnam War lasted until 1971 and ended because there was so much protesting from young people. I know that the VISTA college students hated the war—and every chance they got, they said so. Just before the war, there was another government push to improve the lives of Appalachians and reduce poverty. Programs were started to build roads and bridges to connect small towns with cities. New roads were built between Coulton, other larger towns, and Lexington to encourage manufacturers and businesses to relocate or build. Water and sewer lines were built with local, state, and federal grants. The government thought that the development would increase employment and the economic growth would reduce poverty. The Coulton people were happy with the new roads, the water and sewer lines, and the new businesses, stores, and jobs close by. Improvement in education was important, and vocational schools and community colleges were built in small cities near Lexington for kids who lived in towns like Coulton.

Many Appalachians were excited and positive about the new developments, but they feared the modernization would end up like the War on Poverty and the VISTA programs. Things always seemed to get started but never finished. No wonder poverty never goes away.

In 1971, President Nixon decided to decrease federal funding for welfare programs like Medicaid, food stamps, and Social Security and use the money to fund the Vietnam War, decrease modernization spending, and manage the welfare system better.

The results were positive. Unemployment and poverty rates decreased, coal production increased, and new jobs were created. Most of the changes had no effect on Coulton. We remained isolated and content with the culture we had established.

In 1970, Vietnam protesting across America had reached its peak. Opposition caused violence and destruction everywhere. That year, your mother was born. We named her June because it was her birth month. The unpopular war was finally winding down. Thousands of soldiers never returned, were injured, or suffered from mental health problems. Fortunately, only a couple of boys from Coulton died. Those who were injured healed, but those with trauma didn't.

In 1976, Jimmy Carter from Georgia was elected president. Stories about him revealed that he came from a blue-collar family, knew the value of hard work, and understood the needs of the poor. He worked on welfare reform and work training. He improved the food stamp program, which many of us depended on. Many of his programs to help families and children failed because of politics.

Granny shifted her train of thought here and started talking about her children. She often started one story and switched to another. I thought it might be confusing to my readers, but that was the way she told it.

Your granddaddy and I were very happy living in Coulton and raising our family. All five children remained healthy and got a good education. Max was sixty-nine, Angela was sixty-four, Gregory sixty-one, and Ralph fifty-eight. June, the baby of the family was fifty-four. As you know, your Aunt Angela and your uncles left Coulton after high school to live elsewhere. Your mother was the exception. She stayed and cared for me after Paw-Paw died in 1990. I don't know if I would have survived without her. Your aunt and uncles have good jobs. I wish they had stayed, but I understood why they didn't want to get stuck in Coulton and be dependent on the mine for their jobs. As they were growing up, they would say they wanted better lives for themselves and their children. Because of all five of you, I have fifteen grandchildren and seven great-grandchildren. But enough of the personal stuff. Let's get back to where I left off.

"Where was I?" she asked.

"You had just finished talking about President Carter," I said.

"I remember now."

It was interesting how Granny told her story using the presidents as a guide. I thought it was an ingenious way to recollect events.

After President Carter, President Reagan was elected in 1981. He didn't care for all the welfare programs and felt lowering taxes was the solution to decreasing poverty. I thought it was a good idea if it meant he would get more tax money from the mining company, those who owned the land and didn't pay their taxes, and the rich. Well, his plan didn't work, and it crippled the poor. Again, because we were so isolated from what was going on outside Coulton, his plan had little effect on us. I began to think that our decision to be self-supporting—other than the dependence on the mine company—benefited the town. We had created a culture that had both good and bad, but the good outweighed the bad.

I didn't want Granny to overdo it because of her recent illness, so I suggested taking a break. I went to my room and started editing what Granny had told me. Her memory amazed me, but I noticed she had started losing her train of thought and was a bit redundant. However, I was pleased that the details of her story reinforced information that Great-Granny had told her when she was young, the details revealed in Great-Granny's diaries, and the story Bobbie Joe told.

I decided to tell the Coulton story using the same process Granny used—I would mention each president and explain their plans to eradicate poverty. To make the story more interesting, I would tell stories about my personal life, the lives of others who had lived in Coulton their whole life, and those who came to Coulton later.

I had learned a lot in Bobbie Joe's interview about his life and his family history and how it affected him. I decided to interview my best friend, Sally Mae. She hadn't been born in Coulton, but her family moved here when we were in first grade. Her father was an engineer with the mining company, and her mother was the new one-room schoolhouse teacher. I gave her a call and asked if she wouldn't mind interviewing for the story I was writing. She agreed, and we met the next day at her family's house outside of Coulton, where a bunch of expensive houses had been built for the mine company managers and professional employees. Her father was one of them.

CHAPTER 8
SALLY MAE'S STORY

I was excited about Sally Mae's story. She and her family were outsiders, college-educated, and rich. I thought these three points would give readers a unique perspective.

I arrived at Sally Mae's house at nine in the morning. She answered the door and led me to the living room, which was exceptionally large and filled with expensive furniture and decorations. I scanned the room and immediately recognized that her lifestyle wasn't like that of most of the people I knew, but I liked her because she never put on that she was rich or better than others.

Sally Mae asked if I'd like something to drink.

"No, thank you," I said. "I'd like to get to the interview right away if you don't mind."

"Where do you want me to start?" she asked.

"I know you were only five when you moved to Colton in 1975, and you might not remember a lot about your family before your move."

"You're right, but I can tell you some stories that my mother and father told me."

My family came here from Cleveland, Ohio. My father's parents were immigrants from Italy and came to America in 1890. They settled in Buffalo, NY, but later moved to Cleveland, and that's where my parents and I was born. My grandparents came to the US poor, but they worked hard, built their own house, and started their family. My grandfather worked as a street paver, and my grandmother raised seven children. They struggled their whole lives but vowed they would do all they could to ensure that their children had a better life. My mother's family was from Ireland and settled in America as colonists. Her family came poor as well, but they worked hard and had a much better life than my father's family.

Both of my parents were born in the early seventies, and they met while they were in college. My father became an engineer and my mother a teacher. Dad worked for a steel plant before getting the job in Coulton, and Mom worked in the Cleveland public schools. They decided to move to Coulton when I was five. When I was older, I asked why they made the move. Dad said he was tired of city life and Mom wanted the challenge of teaching children in Appalachia. I was very young and an only child, so it was easy for them to pick up and leave Ohio. I really didn't have much exposure to other places, and Coulton seemed to be a good place to live.

When I met you, I was so happy to have a friend—and I'm even happier that we've remained friends all these years. I remember growing up with you and all the fun we had when we were young. Do you remember the time when you, Bobbie Joe, and I were playing near the old schoolhouse, and he locked himself in the outhouse? He had to kick the door down to get out. When we walked home, we had to keep a safe distance from him because of the smell.

We laughed and laughed, and tears streamed down our cheeks. We both agreed it was the funniest story ever.

"I'll have to remind Bobbie Joe of that story the next time I see him," I said.

We regained our composure, and I asked Sally Mae to describe how she felt growing up in Coulton and how her parents adjusted to the new culture.

I had no family history in Coulton, so it was easy for me. Although I missed my grandparents and other family members, since I was so young, I had no experiences that I missed. Coulton's culture became my culture. I loved going to school and the town celebrations of marriages, birthdays, and holidays. I didn't know anything else, and I was happy. The isolation didn't really have any effect on me until I had to decide about college. The switch from the one-room schoolhouse to a new grade school and high school had prepared me for a career. Like you, I made the decision to go to college and chose UK.

My first year was a challenge. I had never been in such a large setting with thousands of people around me. I didn't think I could make it and thought about dropping out a hundred times. My parents gave me the support I needed, and I stuck it out. I decided to major in business and got a job as soon as I graduated. I've been working as an accountant for two years with a Richmond manufacturer. I like my job a lot because I'm a numbers person.

I realized when I was in college that I could never live in Coulton because there were no career opportunities, and the small-town way of life in the mountains wasn't for me. I'm sure that if I had grown up here, my feelings would be different, but I know that a lot of young people leave and never go back for the same reasons. I wanted to get married, have children, and give them access to a bigger town. I don't question those who live in Coulton or those who have returned, but it's not what I want out of life. I learned a lot about the mountain culture when I lived there, but there was no permanent connection for me. I knew I would have a hard time adapting to a culture that was so far removed and isolated from the mainstream. I guess the biggest drawback was living in a town that has always existed in poverty and is bad-mouthed by outsiders. I visit my parents during the holidays—that's why I'm home now—and that's good enough for me.

Sally Mae stopped. "Are you disappointed by what I told you?" she asked.

"No. I'm grateful you were so candid. It gives me a true picture of how someone who isn't from Coulton and doesn't have our history thinks," I said.

"Would like to hear more?"

"I sure would, and it would be great to hear from your parents too."

"They're home. Let me see if they'd be willing to talk to you."

Sally Mae stepped away from the living room and returned in a few minutes with her parents. I knew Mrs. Gulio because she had been my teacher for a few years, but I had never met Mr. Gulio. I gave Sally's mom a hug and shook her dad's hand.

"Thank you for agreeing to the interview," I said.

"Our pleasure," Mr. Gulio replied. "Where would you like us to begin?"

"Sally Mae told me why you came to Coulton," I said, "so let's begin with your first thoughts about the town and whether you thought you made the right decision."

Mrs. Gulio spoke first.

We chose Coulton because Frank was offered a job at the mine, and I answered an ad in the Harlan News *about a teaching job there. Frank's job came with housing, and I was delighted to be able to work with families in poverty. My first impression after our first visit was concerning. I didn't realize Coulton was so small and immediately discovered that its culture was one of a kind. I was intrigued but not sure it was the right move.*

Mr. Gulio jumped in. "I agreed with Laura at first but then realized that the town wasn't the reason we wanted to move. The challenge of something new was our goal. One of Laura's biggest concerns was Sally Mae's education. We concluded that since Laura would be her teacher, she would be assured of a good education. We decided to give it a two-year trial and rented a house, packed our furniture, and drove to our new home.

"How long did it take before you fully absorbed the cultural change?" I asked.

My job at the mine was new to me, but I had some experience with geology. I'd had no exposure to mountain life and the people's culture. At first, many of the miners were leery of me because I was in management. When they learned I was from the north, they couldn't understand why I wanted to work for a mine company in the middle of nowhere. Before long, though, I gained the miners' confidence by challenging the company and its poor safety regulations. I convinced the company that good safety standards would save them money in the long run if injury insurance claims were reduced. I had solved one of my concerns but needed to work on the other. Since I was an outsider, I had to establish credibility with the townspeople and adapt to a different culture. It took a few years to be accepted. We participated in all the celebrations and were soon welcomed. I think Laura had a lot to do with that.

Laura jumped in—

Being the town's only teacher had a lot to do with our acceptance. Parents recognized that my major concern was their children's education and not their personal family issues. I decided not to get involved in things like the need for a union, safety rules, wages, and benefits. I spoke up if a child needed more educational support or if health was affecting learning.

"What was your impression of the mountain way of life?" I asked Mr. Gulio.

We soon learned about Coulton's long, impoverished history and the struggles its people had endured for generations. Of course, we knew the town's isolated lifestyle was connected with stories about laziness, dependence on welfare, and other negative characteristics. Terms like rednecks, hillbillies, and white trash were spread widely in the north. But before long, we realized that most of the townspeople were hardworking, honest, and friendly.

I think once they got to know us and we them, we accepted one another and became part of the community.

After the interviews, I thanked Sally Mae's parents for giving me a picture of how outsiders saw the mountain people and how they were able to adapt to the mountain culture. Sally Mae walked me to the door.

"See you at the tavern on Saturday," she said.

When I got home, I checked in on Granny. I didn't find her in the living room or kitchen. I went to her bedroom, where Mom was sitting on the bed next to her. She looked up at me with concern.

"How's she doing?" I asked.

"She's been in bed all day, her temperature has returned, and she's having a tough time breathing," she said.

"Should we take her back to the hospital?" I asked, realizing that Granny had not fully recovered from her illness.

"I called Dr. Fielding, and she said she would stop by later after her appointments."

Granny was eighty-three years old but usually seemed as spry as when she was fifty. I hoped that she would be able to fight her illness and live many more years.

I waited for Dr. Fielding for two hours and finally heard a knock on the front door. I opened the door, greeted her, and took her to Granny's bedroom. She gave her a thorough examination and told us that her lungs were congested, and she might have an infection.

"I recommend you call an ambulance and get her back to the hospital in Lexington," she said.

I was so shocked that I could hardly breathe. "I'll call right away. Thank you for coming over," I said.

The EMTs arrived in twenty minutes. They carefully placed Granny in the ambulance and sped away. We followed in my car. When we got to the hospital, Granny was already in a room and on a ventilator. The doctor said that she was in critical condition and needed to be moved to ICU. Mom and I looked at each other, hugged, and watched as the attendants wheeled Granny away.

We spent the night in Granny's room. I didn't sleep at all. I was so worried about Granny that I forgot all about my article for the paper. I thought about Granny's story and all that she had gone through. At around seven in the morning, the sun broke through the clouds, shone through the window, and settled on Granny's face. Mama and I walked toward her bed, and the ventilator and other monitors flashed and beeped. A doctor and nurse rushed into the room. It was too late. She had died peacefully in her sleep. It was December 23, 2023.

We had her transported back to Coulton the next day, and she was taken to the funeral home. Mama and I prepared for the funeral and burial.

Most of the townspeople were at the funeral and cemetery. Granny was well-known, and her "celebration" was well-attended. My aunt and uncles, who only visited during the holidays, made a special trip to Coulton for the funeral and burial. I understood why they had an estranged relationship with Granny and Granddaddy but still couldn't comprehend how they could divorce themselves as family members.

A few days had passed since Granny's death, and Mama and I decided to clean out her bedroom. Mama started with the drawers, and I with the closet. Her dresses were neatly hung, and her shoes were arranged on the floor. There was a cardboard box tucked in the corner of the closet to one side of the clothes rack. I pulled it out. The lid of the box was labeled "MY DIARIES." I was surprised that Granny had kept her own diaries, but now I understood how she was able to remember the detailed information she gave during our interviews. I took the top off the box and picked up the first diary dated 1945-1946. Grandaddy had died in 1940, so Granny would have been six years old. I opened the diary and searched for details about her birth and her father. I thumbed through the pages, stopping when I reached page forty-nine. In the middle of the page, I read, "Mama told me today that my daddy was Patrick. I'm not sure that I was that surprised. After Daddy died, Patrick spent a lot of time at our house. He gave me a lot of attention, and I grew to love him. I remember when he died and how upset Mama was and my feelings about losing him. He was always my best friend."

I closed the diary and looked at Mama. She was busy boxing up Granny's clothes. I walked toward her and asked, "Did you know that Granny's daddy was Patrick?"

She looked at me and said, "Yes."

"Why didn't you tell me?" I asked.

"I had planned to tell you hundreds of times, but I kept putting it off. I thought maybe Granny had already told you, but you didn't want me to know. I also thought you might find out when Granny told you her mama's story," she said.

"I'm upset that you didn't tell me after all these years, and I had to find out after Granny died. I have to admit that I was suspicious after hearing Great Granny's story. I'm relieved that the truth has finally been revealed. Do you know if Granny was upset when she learned the truth?"

"We talked about it a number of times. She had accepted it because she had a good relationship with Patrick, and she never knew her real father," Mom said.

I'm happy that I now know the true story. My only regret is that I had to find out by reading Granny's diary instead of from her. After listening to her story, I wasn't totally surprised that Great-Granny had a relationship with Patrick. Her marriage with Great Grandaddy was difficult. She revealed that their relationship was distant, he paid little attention to their children, and more significantly, he was a drunk.

Mama and I finished cleaning up Granny's belongings and placed a number of boxes in a corner of her room. I took the box that contained her diaries. Afterward, we sat quietly in the living room for a long time. Finally, Mom broke the silence and said she had experienced so many deaths in the past years that she had been able to accept her mama's death as part of life—you're born, and you die. I was more sensitive to Granny's death. It had a tremendous impact on me. I grieved from day one and really didn't get back to my senses for months. I realized that I had a deadline with the *Gazette* but had little interest in continuing to write the article. A couple of days after Granny's death, Mom approached me.

"I know you're distraught about Granny's death and it has affected your interest in finishing your article. I understand that, but I have one question to ask you. What would Granny want you to do?"

I looked at Mom with tears in my eyes and said, "She'd want me to finish it. But I don't know where to start."

"Where did Granny leave off?"

"She had come up with a plan to tell her story in the order of the presidents and their programs on poverty. She was supposed to start up again with George Bush, Sr."

"How about I pick up where Granny left off?" Mom said. "I was twenty when Bush became president and can recall a little bit about his presidency and views on poverty. He became president in 1990, the year Paw-Paw died. Is it okay if I start with my father's death and then talk about George Bush?"

"I think that was Granny's plan, and she would like that," I said.

I was the last of five children and don't know much about my parents' early life. I know they were married in 1955 when Mama was fifteen. Daddy was born in Coulton and worked in the mines his whole life. He liked living here despite all the negativity that outsiders talked about.

He loved Mama dearly and treasured his family. Unlike your aunt and uncles, I had a special relationship with him because I was the youngest and stayed in Coulton. He read a lot and was familiar with politics outside of Coulton. He knew the names of all the organizations and programs that were designed to help Appalachia get out of poverty. I'm afraid his dream was never fulfilled because there are hundreds of towns that still exist in poverty. He was involved with a lot of local, state, and federal projects. He would often come home from the mine and update us on roads that were being built, new sewer and water lines, and new businesses. He was definitely a town leader. He was disappointed when my sister and brothers left Coulton. He always thought they would stay to carry on his work to make things better. He never gave his opinion of why they left.

When I was old enough, I took an interest in his efforts to help Coulton, and I believe that was the special bond we had. He was excited when George Bush was elected president. He hoped he would finally be the answer to his dreams, but that dream was never fulfilled.

His death was sudden. He went to work one day and didn't return. He had a heart attack and died in one of the mine shafts. We were all devastated, and the town had a special ceremony in his honor. Famous politicians and program organizers from all over came to Coulton. He received a medal from the governor to commemorate his service to Coulton and Kentucky. Mama and I were so proud of him. I still think of him and all the work he did to make Appalachia a better place to live. Granny and I were upset that your aunt and my uncles didn't come to the funeral. There's a disturbing reason why your aunt and uncles left Coulton and never returned. I'll tell you the whole story when you interview me.

I looked at Mom and saw a gleam in her eyes. She never knew her daddy, but I was sure she would have loved him and he, her.

Now, my recollection of George H. Bush.

If I recall correctly, his claims to fame were the American Disabilities Act and the revised Civil Rights Act. The new laws were felt in Coulton. Because the minimum hourly wage was increased, the mine had to increase the pay for workers. President Bush didn't do much for the poor, and the poverty rate rose a lot, especially in Appalachia.

I know your Paw-Paw would not have been happy with President Bush and would have been fully involved in protesting against him. I was twenty and didn't fully understand the impact of increased poverty rates but knew there were a lot more people who did. That's about it. You might want to write more about the presidents that followed Bush.

I thanked Mama for taking Granny's place but knew a whole segment of her story would be missed. I decided that I would write about the presidents where Mom left off.

CHAPTER 9
PRESIDENTS AND POVERTY STORIES

I PICKED UP THE STORY ABOUT PRESIDENTS where Granny and Mom left off, realizing I couldn't replace Granny's real-life storytelling. I would have to do a lot of research to know what each president after President Bush did or didn't do to help alleviate poverty.

The next president after President Bush was President Clinton. He took office in 1993. I read that during his presidency, he created twenty-two million jobs, lowered the unemployment rate, raised educational standards, and doubled education and training investments. He was able to lower welfare dependence to the lowest level in thirty years. He helped the poor, especially Black people, by reducing poverty and raising incomes. I was encouraged by all I read about President Clinton, but what I really wanted to know was how he helped the people in Coulton. After some more research, I learned that he extended a healthcare program called CHIP (Children's Health Insurance Program) and increased funding for the food stamp program for women and children called WIC (Women, Infants, and Children). I was familiar with both programs but didn't know if families in Coulton benefited from them. I learned that a lot of families were dependent on the programs, but I didn't know to what extent. I decided that as long as the poor were helped in some way, I was happy.

I hadn't planned to get so involved in politics, but I realized that if poverty was going to be reduced, politics had to play a crucial role. I decided to limit my research on presidents and poverty and include only the most relevant information, especially how Coulton was affected. I hadn't paid much attention to politics over the years and felt that Daddy would be proud of my writing about presidents.

The president following President Clinton was George W. Bush. He became the forty-third president in 2001. During his term, the policies that had an impact on families and children in poverty included a huge tax cut, education reform, Medicare improvements, and housing assistance. The tax cuts put more money in the hands of the poor, and education reform gave more poor children a route out of poverty. The education law known as No Child Left Behind had a significant impact on the schools in Coulton. Children who often fell behind in reading and math were targeted. They were given more teacher support, and their reading and math skills improved. Many parents were happy with the law and saw their children learn more and become happier.

After two terms, Barack Obama replaced President Bush in 2009. President Obama was the first African American president in American history and became a champion of the poor. His policy to create a job program helped low-income families earn more money. The most significant program, The Affordable Care Act, provided health insurance for low-income families and patient protection. His programs also improved school nutrition and provided free lunch programs. President Obama's policies had a direct effect on families in Coulton. Many families didn't have health insurance, and the new provisions for nutrition and health provided money for breakfast and summer food support.

Donald J. Trump followed President Obama in 2017. He began his four terms by concentrating on unemployment, family income, and poverty, but his presidency was clouded by the COVID pandemic. At the beginning of his term, the unemployment rate was low, but it increased dramatically when COVID hit. The pandemic caused food insecurity and an increase in food stamp needs. Poverty became widespread and hit Coulton hard. During the three-year period, Coulton experienced more than twenty deaths and hundreds of infected children and older adults. COVID had a tremendous personal effect on me because it took Granny's life.

Joe Biden was elected president in 2020. One of his most significant achievements for the poor was the extension of "Obama Care." In addition to the Obama provisions, the program reinforced protection for Americans with preexisting conditions. The provision was extremely important to Coulton families because of black lung disease. The law also helped the poor with the expansion of Medicaid and affordable health insurance.

The research I did on presidents and poverty was rewarding. I had a better understanding of how their policies and programs affected all of America and the Coulton poor. I was sure that Granny would have offered a more personal accounting with a lot more color.

When I finished the presidents' stories, I decided to call Ben. I wanted to give him an update and find out when and how he planned on advertising and marketing the story.

"I'm happy you called," he said when he answered. "I was just thinking about you. I'm sorry to hear that your grandmother has passed. I hope you're doing okay."

"Her death was such a shock, and I'm still trying to accept it while staying focused on writing the article," I said.

"If you need more time, please tell me," Ben said.

"No, writing the article helps me keep my mind occupied," I said. "So, what are your plans for sharing the story with the public?"

"I want to start advertising next week and give snippets of it to generate interest and a following."

"Well, I've finished five chapters, and I think you could pull from them," I said.

"Sounds good. Send me the chapters, and I'll condense them for printing. When do you think the whole story will be finished?"

"I'm shooting for mid-January. Next week is Christmas, so that should give me enough time," I said.

"Okay, please take care. Let me know if you need more time."

I turned off my phone and sat down to write.

CHAPTER 10
MOM'S STORY

I found Mom in the dining room looking at family photos. "I've been looking for you. How are you doing?" I asked.

"Filled with nostalgia," she said.

"Is this a good time for you to tell me your story?"

"How about we start tomorrow? I'm tired right now and want to take a nap."

I knew Mom was still grieving Granny's death, so postponing her interview might be best. I decided to see how she felt in the morning.

The next morning, Mom approached me and asked if I was ready to start her interview.

"I think telling my story would be good for me," she said.

The earliest time I can remember is when I was five. Max was nineteen, Angela was fifteen, Greg was eleven, and Ralph was eight. We had moved into our own house and no longer depended on the mining company's rental. It was a happy time for the whole family. The new house had four bedrooms, a big backyard, and was within walking distance to town. We would have a barbecue every weekend during the summer and would play all kinds of outdoor games. We even had an above-ground swimming pool. Aunt Angela played with me all the time, and I loved every minute of it. One time, I got a cramp in my leg and was drowning. I was gasping for air when Angela pulled me out of the pool. She gave me mouth-to-mouth and saved my life.

I remember my first day of school. The big yellow bus pulled up in front of our house, and we all climbed in. Max had graduated high school and was working in the mine. Angela was in tenth grade, Greg was in junior high, and Ralph and I were in elementary school. The schools were located next to each other, so we all took the same bus to school and back home. There were about twenty kids on the bus who lived in various parts of the county. The back-and-forth ride was long. It took more than an hour each way. We got on the bus at six thirty in the morning and got home at five thirty. For a first grader, it was hard. I slept to and from school every day.

There were a lot of parents who complained about the long ride and would rather have sent their kids to the old one-room schoolhouse in Coulton. All the town schools were combined by the county in 1965, so there was no chance that would ever happen. Also, the old school had burned down, and Coulton never had a high school anyway. When the Civil Rights Act was passed along with the federal government movement to make Appalachia more modern, the new county school concept became a needed reality.

When Max was five years old, he started in the new elementary school. There were protests all over the county about towns losing their neighborhood schools and the long bus rides. Even the Coulton townspeople were upset. But as time passed, most parents accepted the change and recognized that the new county concept was better for all children. There were more educational, social, and athletic advantages and more opportunities for white and Black children, whether poor or rich.

The plan to modernize Appalachia affected Coulton. There were better country roads and highways, and there was electricity, natural gas, and indoor plumbing. Retail stores and more jobs helped some get out of poverty. In the past, local, state, and federal governments tried to pass and implement a number of different laws and programs to reduce poverty. They would work for a while, but often politics, control, and greed won out. Looking back, we are better off now than we ever were. The new county schools and modernization have given hope to the people of Appalachia and Coulton. That hope has helped some families get out of poverty and have better lives.

Mom paused and looked at me. "I'm sorry for getting off track and talking about the Civil Rights Act and the modernization plan," she said, "but I think it's important for your readers to know about our feelings. School was important to all families, as was finally getting improved roads, indoor plumbing, and clean water. We went through tough times for generations, but we never gave in, and Coulton is better for it today. Now let's see . . . where were we? Oh yes, I had just started first grade."

As I moved up through the grades, the bus ride got easier, and I didn't need to sleep both ways anymore. My family and friends celebrated all the town events. I loved school and often thought about what I would like to do after high school. It was a long way off, but it was something that was always in the back of my mind. I had a lot of friends at school—white, Black, poor, and rich. We got along well, and to this day I still have some of those friendships.

When I was in fourth grade, Angela graduated from high school and my cherished bus rides with her ended. I latched on to Greg and Ralph, and they became Angela's replacements. Max had quit the mine after his accident and moved to Nashville. He became a cook in a local diner. Angela joined Max and left Coulton as soon as she graduated. She had become a talented folk singer and guitar player and hoped that Nashville would give her a start in the country music world. I missed her tremendously. She'd left so suddenly without telling anyone why. It hurt me a lot that she didn't even say goodbye to me. I hoped that someday I would find out the real reason she left.

I was disappointed when Max left but took Angela's move harder. I couldn't understand why anyone would leave Coulton to go to a big city far away from family, friends, and the security of home. At the time, I didn't realize a lot of young people were leaving Appalachia in search of better lives. Coal mining was up and down, safety was still a big concern, and many were lured to northern cities for greater opportunities.

I mentioned earlier that Max had a mining accident and was left with only one good leg. I had just finished baking a pie and remember being startled by the mine's emergency siren. I ran out the front door and looked toward the mine and saw a black cloud of smoke. It meant only one thing— there was a cave-in in the underground mine. It was less than a mile from our house, and I ran toward it as fast as I could. When I got there, a fireman explained what happened and said that three miners were still inside. I looked around at the miners who had escaped. I couldn't find Max. The mine superintendent approached and told me that Max and two others were stuck in one of the shafts. He said they knew their location but were unable to reach them. The firefighters decided to try getting to them through a safety ladder opening above the mine. It took more than an hour for them to reach the opening. Then they had to dig down five feet to get to the lid. A firefighter was lowered, and he found the three miners. All three were unconscious and would have died if the rescue had taken any longer. Oxygen tanks were lowered down to the miners, and they were revived. Two were uninjured, but Max's leg was crushed. He was lifted out and rushed to a Lexington hospital. I rode with him and prayed he would be okay. He was in surgery for three hours. An orthopedic surgeon approached me afterward and told me that everything went well but he would need a lot of physical therapy and would walk with a limp. I was happy he didn't lose his leg and wouldn't be working in the mine anymore. Six months later, Max had healed, and his limp was almost unnoticeable. He decided to leave Coulton and move to Nashville. He had always wanted to be a chef and thought that the move would give him the opportunity.

Mom said she thought Max's story would show how dangerous the mines were and what families went through whenever they heard a siren.

"I'm glad you told the story because my readers will want to know about the fears families had for loved ones who worked in the mines. Also, you answered my question about why Max left Coulton. It wasn't the usual story about wanting a better life," I said. And then I asked Mama a question about something that had bothered me for a long time. "Do you know why Angela left so suddenly after graduating from high school?" I knew Mama was sensitive about it, and I didn't want to upset her.

"I do, and it's a very disturbing story that I've been heartbroken about since I found out. I hope you aren't too upset after hearing it. It has also had a drastic effect on your brothers," she said.

The year I graduated from high school, I decided to go to Nashville to see Max and Angela. Max had been there for six years and Angela for four. Max had become a chef in an expensive restaurant, and Angela was singing and playing guitar in bars around town. Max was very happy with his work. I met him at the restaurant, and he talked about his job and his girlfriend— he had met a woman, and they were planning to get married.

I asked how Angela was, and he said not well. He said she was struggling and living gig to gig. At that point, tears came to his eyes, and he said he needed to tell me something about Angela that he had never told anyone, including Mom. I couldn't imagine what he was going to tell me. He said he knew it was going to be hard for me to accept and comprehend, but it had to do with Daddy.

When Angela was fifteen, she told Max that Daddy kissed and touched her. She told him that she was frightened and ran from him. She said it had happened only one time, but he wasn't sure about that. Daddy apologized to her a thousand times, but she could never forgive him.

When she graduated from high school, she called Max and asked if she could stay with him. While she was there, she told him about the incident. He asked if she had told their mom, and she said she hadn't because she was embarrassed, didn't want Daddy to get trouble, and didn't want Mama to have to deal with it. She felt it was her fault.

I was paralyzed after hearing the story. Now I understood why Angela had left so suddenly and never said goodbye. She couldn't or didn't want to tell me what had happened.

I thanked Max for telling me what had happened to Angela and told him how difficult it must have been for him to hold the secret for all these years. I was relieved that I finally knew the reason Angela left. I always thought it might have been something I did. I decided to talk to her. It would be good for both of us, and I thought it might relieve her guilt and renew our relationship.

Max and I had planned to listen to Angela sing and play at a local bar that evening. She knew I was in town, so Max called and told her our plan. I hadn't seen her in two years, and I knew the meeting would be awkward for both of us. We met her at the bar and listened to her performance. It was impressive. When she finished, we greeted each other with an uncomfortable hug. We had a drink and talked about our childhood. I said nothing about the incident, wanting to wait for a more appropriate time and place. I asked her if she would like to have breakfast in the morning. She agreed.

We met at a small diner and sat in a secluded booth. We had some small talk before I decided to approach her about the incident. I was uncomfortable and didn't know how she would react to me bringing it up. I finally overcame my apprehension and blurted out that Max told me about the incident with Daddy. She looked me straight in the eyes and asked if he had ever tried anything with me. When I said he hadn't, she said she was relieved because that had bothered her since she left. She said she had gotten over the incident as best she could and was happy I knew about it. She told me she missed me and was glad we could be big sister and little sister again. With tears flowing down our cheeks, we stood and held each other tightly for a long time. That was the beginning of the strong, renewed relationship we now have.

When I got back to Coulton, I avoided Daddy and kept my distance from Mom. I didn't want to bring the incident up to either of them. It was now my secret.

Mom continued her story a couple of days later.

I finished grade school with Greg and Ralph and went on to junior high. I didn't like seventh and eighth grade and looked forward to high school. I had become a good cheerleader and became the captain in my senior year. I liked sports and enjoyed cheering for all the teams.

In eleventh grade, I met Tim. He was the quarterback on the varsity football team. We went to all the high school events and suspected we would stay together after high school. We went to our senior prom together and graduated with honors. Tim was offered a college football scholarship but injured his shoulder in his final football game and never recovered from the injury. He decided to stay in Coulton and work in the mine. I had thought about being a nurse but knew I would have to leave Coulton and Tim if I did, so I stayed.

I thought it was a suitable time for a break and said to Mom, "How about we meet back here around two?"

I wanted to touch base with Ben and ask about his advertising and marketing plan for the article, so I gave him a call.

"Everything okay?" he asked.

"Everything's fine. We're still grieving Granny's death. She was such a big part of our family. But I've come to grips with things and thought we should discuss your advertising and marketing plan."

"Christmas is only a week away, and we need to have the plan ready to go by then," he said. "I've given it a lot of thought, and I think we should advertise your article in the Saturday Review Human Interest section."

"We should start with a brief description of my great-grandparents' emigration to America. We might be able to attract readers with family who made the same journey," I said.

"That's a great idea. Let's go with it. Send the piece to me, and we'll get it ready for publication."

I had to make the piece engaging so that readers would continue to follow the story each week. I thought about *Coal Town Stories* as the title and wondered if it would capture the eyes of the readers. I concluded that the title might be of interest to families from Appalachia and specifically Eastern Kentucky. I wanted to introduce the story with a question and wrote a few ideas down on paper before deciding on "Have you ever thought about what life would be like living in a small Kentucky coal town?" The follow-up would be, "Join us as we begin telling the story of a family who's lived in a coal town for four generations. Read how the family struggled over the years, survived many trials and tribulations, and were successful in adapting to an unknown culture."

I texted the lead to the story to Ben, and he responded immediately. "Go with it," he said. I wrote the introduction to the story around the question and answer and emailed it to him.

It was close to two o'clock when I returned to the living room. Mom was sitting next to the window, staring into space.

"Are you ready?" I asked.

"I've been waiting. Let's get going," she replied without skipping a beat.

After your daddy and I graduated from high school, we decided to stay in Coulton and raise our family. Mama and Daddy were living in the family home, and they asked us to move in. Mama and I planned the wedding, and on August 10, 1988, your daddy and I were married. There was a huge celebration. Most of the town came because they went to Tim's football games every Friday night. The games were a big part of Coulton's culture and not going was considered a sin. Our wedding was held in the mining company barn just like everyone else. There was lots of food and drink. Granny had baked a cake and was so proud that I was getting married and living in Coulton. Angela and your uncles came but left the next day. Daddy was overjoyed about me getting married, but he kept his distance from Angela and my brothers. Your daddy and I moved into Granny's house, and that's where we started our married life. Paw-Paw got a job in the mine, and I got an RFD job with the post office. The first couple of years, we saved money to start a family.

Willie was born in the spring of 1990. I was happy that he was healthy, and your daddy was proud that his first child was a boy. I think when the firstborn is a boy, the father assumes he has a friend for life and is happy the family name will continue. It didn't matter to me if I had a boy or girl, just as long as there were no health problems.

Just before Willie was born, I took a leave from the post office but was back to work in three months. I was fortunate that Granny lived with us and could care for Willie. Your daddy was promoted to a new job and no longer had to go into an underground mine. I remember the day he told me. I was so happy. I bought a bottle of cheap champagne and we celebrated. We had never tasted it before, and after a smell and sip, we quickly poured it down the kitchen sink and celebrated with sweet iced tea instead.

We enjoyed Willie so much that we had Paul in 1992. He was as healthy as Willie and a lot more work from day one. He wouldn't sleep, eat, or stop crying. I was concerned, but Granny said he was colicky and that Greg was the same. Granny eventually got everything under control, and your daddy and I thanked her every day.

By 1992, Coulton had recovered from the early recession in 1980, and coal was mined twenty-four seven. Tim was gone a lot, and I was busy with my job. Mama took care of Willie and Paul. I thought life was surprisingly good.

New state and federal programs were started to reduce poverty. The old programs never worked, so we were counting on the new ones. Hardcore poverty in Appalachia and Coulton had become a way of life for generations and an accepted part of our culture. We were surprised when we saw that some of the new programs were successful. The food stamp law was improved, housing support was better, and the Medicaid program money increased. However, many families continued to struggle even with the new programs.

A major concern for Appalachia and Coulton was the new ways coal was being mined. Underground mining had been used for years, but with modern technology, the strip and mountaintop mining became more popu-

lar. Mines were dug with new equipment, and more jobs were created. The disadvantages of strip and mountaintop mining were soon discovered. Coal sulfur would flow down the mountainside and poison the water, farmland was lost, timber production was cut, and flooding became a problem. The positives of a cheaper, more productive, and safer way of mining soon became negatives.

In 1993, the worst tragedy of all struck Coulton . . . a tornado. The mine sirens started blaring throughout the valley. It wasn't the short beeping sound of a cave-in but the long pulsating siren that only sounded when there was a weather alert. I quickly turned on the TV and caught the tail end of an emergency alert for Harlan County. The weather reporter didn't say which towns would be affected. He didn't have to. I looked out the window and saw a dark funnel-shaped cloud heading straight for Coulton. Tim was working and hopefully safe in the underground mine. Willie was in a safe place at school, and Granny was with me. I helped her to the basement and ran outside to check on our neighbors. We were the only house with a basement, so I got as many neighbors as I could find to our basement. I ran back outside for more neighbors and spotted the tornado coming closer and heading straight for Coulton. I ran back inside, slammed the front door shut, raced to the basement door, and hurried to a corner where Granny sat in fear. The wind and rain lasted for a few minutes and then all was calm. I walked up the basement stairs and opened the door. The roof was completely blown off. The neighbors followed me and walked to what was left of their houses. Most of them were in the same condition as ours. Everyone was terrified, crying, and in shock. I thought about Tim and Willie and prayed they were safe.

Tim got home an hour after the storm hit. He walked toward what was left of our house and hugged Granny and me. We have a big job ahead of us, he said. I asked if all the miners were safe, and he said there had been close to fifty miners huddled back to back. They all left the mine together and walked toward their homes. I asked how the town looked, and he said the courthouse was still standing. I asked about the houses where the rich lived, and he said they weren't damaged and the houses up the hollow were still standing, but the miners' houses and the town buildings got the most damage.

In less than an hour, fire engines, ambulances, and state and federal officials were on site. FEMA trailers were brought in and hooked up with electricity the following day. Max was bused to the top of the street and walked to what was left of our house. We stood in the front yard that was cluttered with pieces of the roof and held each other tightly. The Red Cross gave us blankets, food, and clothing and found us housing for the night. We were assigned to a family in the hollow. We walked through town and were shocked to see all the destruction. That image has stayed with me.

We walked up the hollow and looked for the house to which we were assigned. When we got there, an elderly man and woman greeted us with open arms. They had prepared a hot meal and made beds for us on the living room floor. We were so worn out and still in shock. I thought our new residence was like a fancy hotel. There were close to forty families that lost their houses and belongings. Luckily, no one was killed or injured. We were all put up in houses owned by the rich and the poor. Coulton had showed its bright light again!

In the morning, we had breakfast with Mr. and Mrs. Rider and thanked them for their hospitality. We walked through town and headed toward our house. We were surprised that the damage wasn't as bad as we thought.

We knew that the townspeople would work together and bring Coulton to life again. Clean-up had already started. The mining company had bulldozers and dump trucks in place. Power, gas, and water companies were on site repairing their lines. Everything was happening so quickly. Neighbors from all three sides of the town joined in and began clearing away debris and sawing fallen trees and branches.

Some families left and fled north to stay with friends or relatives, but FEMA assigned trailers to the families that stayed. When the trailers were set, all the families that had been left homeless were now living on a nearby farm. Many of the stores were still standing but not open for business. It took more than a year before everything was rebuilt and back to normal. We lived in the trailer for three months until a new roof was put on our house. We had salvaged most of our personal things like pictures, furniture, and household items and stored them in storage units provided by FEMA.

When I look back, there's one thing that really stuck out. When times are tough, and you think all is lost, our town always came together to help each other. The color of your skin and how much money you had didn't matter when your neighbors needed help. Coulton showed its true colors. That's why I love Coulton! We continued to have our ups and downs for the next couple of years, but we made it through because we are mountain people and recognize the value of helping each other.

After the tornado, the federal government reported that Appalachia was one of the poorest places in the US. Poverty had become one of the most persistent concerns of the country. The gap between the rich and poor grew, welfare benefits decreased, unemployment was widespread, and healthcare improvements were at a standstill.

Mine safety regulations were overlooked, and many miners were injured or died because of the company's negligence. Many workers suffered from disabilities and became dependent on addictive drugs like OxyContin and Vicodin prescribed by mountain doctors. Compounding all the problems, *the need for coal declined and jobs were permanently lost. Many families moved to northern cities to seek work and a better life.*

A positive welcome was rare. The mountain families brought their customs, language, a low level of education, and disease with them. Rumors about their backwardness, poor work ethic, and dependence on government programs followed them. Names like hillbillies, rednecks, and white trash spread wherever the mountain people settled. Many families gave up and returned to the coal towns to face poverty all over again. A few families left Coulton to explore the supposed benefits of the big cities. I often thought the reasons we were shunned had to do with not knowing or understanding our culture. True, we were isolated and wanted to keep a lifestyle that was more community and family-oriented. Our language, music, religion, celebrations, and other customs were preserved through generations, and most of us did not want to give them up.

The mine company controlled us, absentee landowners didn't pay their share of the taxes, politicians usually got their way, and the state and federal government tried to change much of what we cherished and disguise it as modernization to reduce poverty. Through the years, many programs were tried. Some were successful, but many failed to reverse the downward spiral of poverty and all the negatives that came with it. Many of the townspeople had accepted our way of life and were simply happy with the way we were.

In 1994, Katy arrived. Her two brothers adored her from day one. She followed them everywhere, and they loved it. We had become a tight-knit, happy family and enjoyed all the positives that Coulton offered. Willie had started second grade, and my daily chores and raising three children became less demanding. My post office job helped with paying the bills, especially when the mine slowed or shut down. Shopping centers popped up overnight in larger cities close to Coulton. The new highways were safe and helped speed up drives to the cities and transportation to the county schools.

Tourism brought a lot of outsiders to the mountains. I was always suspect that they came to see a backward culture—families in run-down shacks, a flock of barefooted kids, pregnant woman, and shiftless men. Now and then a few groups would come to Coulton and were disappointed that they didn't see what they expected. On the contrary, Coulton always showed its best side—kept housing, family celebrations, church functions, and friendliness to all. I was so proud of my town and was thankful we never left.

Between 1994 and 2000, a major concern among all Appalachian people was the effect that the three types of mining had on the environment. With the advent of new machinery and technology, underground mining was used less. Strip and mountaintop mining became more widely used. It wasn't as expensive, there were fewer injuries and deaths, and less manpower was needed. The major concerns were poor water quality, loss of timber and farming land, floods, and landscape ugliness. Our concerns were brought to the mine companies, landowners, and politicians. Their response was always the same—you can't get in the way of progress, jobs are still available, and most are benefiting from it in one way or another. We weren't dumb. We knew that power, control, and greed were the motivators. Environmentalists latched on to our concerns and tried to assert their power and influence when possible, but the problems are still a major concern today.

In 1996, John was born. He was healthy and a bundle of joy.

Most Coulton families continued to struggle with poverty, but the bond that had developed among us through the years prevailed. Family and friend loyalty was foremost. The majority of the families respected one another and believed in human dignity, social justice, fairness, and compassion. Because

Coulton's population was so small, and everyone supported one another, we stuck together. When a family or an individual was in need, the church and other families reached out to help. A personal helping hand guided many of the families through rough times.

The church played an integral part in keeping the faith. Its support and guidance were beacons of light to those who had given up on our way of life and had no place to turn. Poverty was usually the primary reason for psychological and emotional problems. The image publicized by outsiders affected individuals in town, and depression and withdrawal often resulted in drug and alcohol addiction and suicide.

There were a lot of positives that came from our cultural history. Many had overcome feelings of hopelessness and developed a vision of prosperity. Your father and I always looked on the positive side of things and worked hard to overcome adversities, and that's how we raised our family. No family or individual is perfect, but when someone is down, you should try to pick that person up. Our family is no exception.

There has been plenty of good but also some bad. There have been incidents over the years that we are not proud of, but we have accepted them, dealt with them, and moved on.

Mom sat back in her chair and gazed out the window with a sigh of relief. It was a tough story to tell, and I'm sure it brought back memories she had long forgotten. I was pleased to hear Mom's story about the personal side of families and individuals adversely affected by poverty. It made me realize that our family worked hard for generations to maintain a balanced life dealing with good and bad. The revelation about Angela was startling. It had an adverse effect on the entire family. I was shocked at what my granddaddy had done. His behavior affected

Angela the most, but it was difficult for all of us to accept. I was happy to learn that Angela no longer felt guilty, Great-Granny had accepted the incident as best she could and had renewed her relationship with her daughter, and Max had gotten rid of the burden he had carried for years.

I thought about Mom's story and how it affected me. There were a few incidents I thought about from time to time, and I reminded myself to save those for my story.

Christmas was a few days away, and we would celebrate the holiday at our house. Granny, Mama, and I loved Christmas because it was a time when families got together to share their love for one another. Of course, the birth of Christ was foremost, but getting and giving a gift or two was always a pleasure.

Bobbie Joe came to mind as I was wrapping Sally Mae's gift. She and I had exchanged every year since we first met. We knew each other so well that we were never disappointed in what we got. I had never given a Christmas present to Bobbie Joe and contemplated whether I should this year. We had only been together a couple of times since I returned, and each time was positive. What he told me about his family history, his feelings about life in Coulton, and his desire to better himself were very personal. His confiding in me was special. I wondered what he might like as a gift.

Christmas Day had arrived, and my brothers and their families arrived right on time. Katy had moved to New York and couldn't make it. She was interested in fashion and had an internship with a company. She was extremely talented, and we were all very proud of her. We had prepared our traditional holiday dinner—country ham, mashed potatoes, biscuits and gravy, fried okra, and apple pie for dessert. We sat at the extended dining room table with card tables placed along the wall. Daddy sat at the head of the table, and we joined hands in prayer. Afterward, we exchanged gifts. Mom handed me a gift from Granny. The box had a red ribbon around it that was tied in Granny's customary bow. I opened the box carefully and took out a book. *Uneven Ground . . . Appalachia Since 1945* by Ronald D. Eller. I was surprised that Granny had given me a book that would help me with my article. She was a remarkable woman!

I put the book back in the box, and we continued chatting over the meal.

Paul brought up the time that Willie had gotten so drunk that he walked into the wrong house on the way home from the tavern. All the mining company's houses looked the same, so it was a legitimate mistake and funny until old man Harold got hold of his shotgun and peppered Willie with buckshot. Dr. Rampart worked for hours with a tweezer, pulling the shots out of Willie's behind one at a time. The story spread all over Coulton and was talked about not just in our family but in many others to this day. Other stories were told, and we laughed at each one. The holiday ended with goodbyes and hugs.

It was still early in the evening, so I gave Sally Mae a call and asked if she would like to come over and exchange gifts. She said she was busy, but we could get together tomorrow.

I had made the decision to give Bobbie Joe a gift. "Are you busy?" I asked when I called him.

"Yes, Sally Mae and I are exchanging gifts at her house," he said.

I was in shock. I didn't know that he and Sally were chummy enough to exchange gifts. Quickly, my shock turned to jealousy. I had assumed that Bobbie Joe was my best friend. To learn that he and Sallie Mae were friends surprised me. I knew there was always the possibility that he would be interested in someone else, but did it have to be Sally Mae? I snapped out of my funk. "Okay, maybe we can get together over the weekend," I said.

"Sure, that sounds good. How about I drop over Saturday evening?"

"How about seven?"

"See you then," he said.

I felt sick after I got off the phone with Bobbie Joe. Had I taken him for granted and thought he would always be mine even though I never gave him any indication I liked him? How could I even consider giving him a Christmas gift now?

There was a knock on my bedroom door. Mom opened it and wanted to know when I planned to continue the interview.

"Let's start in the morning. I had a long day and want to get to bed early," I said. I didn't give her the real reason.

I was up early the next day, and Mom was waiting for me in the kitchen. She looked at me and said, "I think I left off just after John was born."

I just turned twenty-seven, had three children ranging in ages from one to eleven, had a full-time job, and was as happy as could be. With our two incomes, we were doing better than most Coulton families. I would say we had escaped poverty and functioned like a middle-class family. There was always a fear that we wouldn't have the income to enjoy the life we had.

Life in Coulton didn't change much from 1997 to 2001. A majority of the families in town lived from paycheck to paycheck and struggled to meet their bills. Despite their poverty, many continued to value the culture that had been handed to them. Celebrations were still a big part of our lives, along with our faith in God, and with our support of one another, we knew we would survive. The mine company continued to influence most people's lives. Without that weekly paycheck, many more townspeople would have left. State and local governments continued to come up with laws and plans to improve our lot. Again, some worked, some didn't. I began to recognize that as presidents, governors, and local politicians changed, so did their efforts. If a political party changed, then the focus changed. It was an uphill battle, and poor people were the victims.

The environment was the foremost concern to Appalachia and the people in Coulton. Water continued to be poisoned, land was constantly eroded, agriculture was in decline, timber production had fallen, and the landscape was ugly. We voiced our concerns when possible, and there was some effort to help, but the help was minimal. Money always won out.

Stories about our negative lifestyle continued to be told. Even though the tourism push became more popular, visitors walked away with a negative view of Appalachia, and that's something that I think will never change. I encouraged the town officials to capitalize on our uniqueness and put our best foot forward to show outsiders the positives of our lifestyle. Most agreed with my idea, and we became known as a small mountain town whose positive attitude has promoted a better way of life.

On September 11, 2001, America was shaken by the terrorist attack in New York City. You would think that the attack would go unnoticed in a small Appalachian town like Coulton. It didn't. We were glued to our TVs the day it happened and many weeks thereafter. When I look back on that day, I realize the reason we felt the tragedy so hard—it was because Coulton has always been very patriotic. Boys fought in all the wars. Some were injured, left with psychological problems, or didn't come home. Families grieved their losses but never wavered in their commitment to our country. Our family was fortunate because we didn't lose anyone in any of the wars since WWII. The veterans' monument that was erected in the town square after the Vietnam War is a tribute and testimonial to the families that did.

I was carrying my sixth child when the towers were struck. I was due the following week, but that didn't happen. Maureen Healy McGuire was born the day after 9/11. I went into labor early that day, and she was born late that evening. I always thought she came early because of the effect the terrorist attack had on me. I was totally distraught and angry. You were born with a cold and had to be nursed carefully for six months. You rebounded from your illness and became a strong and independent child.

Willie had turned thirteen and entered high school. I talked to him often about his future. He had no intention of leaving Coulton but was adamant about not working in the mine and had given thought to owning land and raising cattle and growing tobacco. I was pleased with his interest in agriculture but especially elated that he wanted to live in Coulton.

The rest of the kids were in grade school and doing well. We were pleased that all our children recognized the importance of education. I wondered if any of them would go to college. No one in the previous generations did. Tim and I continued to work as hard as we could, and Granny was always at our side to help.

Coulton's population continued to decline as families left for jobs and a better life. The mine company was still producing a small amount of coal in Coulton's only underground mine. The miners and their families were always concerned that the mine would close and jobs would be gone forever. Governmental initiatives to decrease poverty and offer a better life were again introduced. Because the projects were always hit or miss, confidence in them had eroded. The backbone of our town was its solidarity and the culture that had emerged over the years. I often wondered when the initiatives would end, and the proponents finally realize that we like who we are and don't want to change.

As long as mining existed, Coulton would always be threatened by its negative effects. There was really no other option and the mining companies knew it. If the mine closed, Coulton would become a ghost town. The movement to go green was a stark reality that might cause the town to go under. Natural gas, solar energy, nuclear power plants, and electric for businesses, homes, and cars had grown in popularity because they had less carbon emission that affected the climate. I shuddered to think about the future if coal were no longer needed.

Mom paused and took a break. I was impressed with her knowledge of the outside world and how coal mining was Coulton's lifeline. Without it, there was no future.

New Year's was a few days away, and Coulton always had a big celebration. There was even a simulated NYC ball drop from the courthouse bell tower. I had planned to see Bobbie Joe on Saturday but was going to cancel. I was still irritated that Sally Mae had deceived me by not telling me she was seeing Bobbie Joe behind my back. I remembered that she and I were meeting tonight to exchange Christmas gifts. I thought about canceling but didn't.

Mom returned, and I asked if we could continue our interview tomorrow. I didn't want to tell her why.

Sally Mae showed up at seven o'clock with a big smile on her face. I asked myself if she was gloating because she had stolen my boyfriend and then couldn't believe what I had just thought. *He's not your boyfriend.*

We sat in the living room, had some small talk, and exchanged our gifts. I always tried to personalize my gift, but I struggled this year. I decided on a gold necklace with a ruby pendant. I knew she loved jewelry, and rubies were her favorite gem. She handed me my gift, and I opened it slowly. I couldn't imagine what could be in such a large, flat box. I unfolded the tissue wrapping and pulled out a large, framed picture of Bobbie Joe, Sally Mae, and me. The picture had been taken when we were in high school, and I had forgotten all about it.

"Where did you get this?" I asked.

"Well, Bobbie Joe had the picture blown up and gave it to me the night you called," she said.

I was so embarrassed that I must have turned ten shades of red. I didn't mention anything about my jealous thoughts and gave her a big sisterly hug. After she left, I called Bobbie Joe to ask if he was still coming by on Saturday night.

"I certainly am," he replied.

I knew at that moment that my Christmas present to him was the right one.

Mom and I continued our interview early the next morning. "You look happier than you did last night," she said.

I didn't say a thing.

Not much exciting happened until Willie graduated from high school in 2007. He bummed around town for a couple of months, trying to figure out his future. He burst into the house one Saturday afternoon and told your daddy and me that he was going to be a farmer. Our first question was where he was going to get the money to buy land, equipment, and livestock. He also had no farming experience. He asked us if we would consider taking a loan out on our house for five thousand dollars because Mr. Willis was selling his five-acre farm with the house, barn, and all his equipment, and he said he'd teach Willie the ropes. All Willie needed was a down payment.

Daddy and I looked at each other with skepticism. We said we'd sleep on it and let him know. After a few days, we gave Willie our okay. Our biggest concern was how he would make enough money to pay Mr. Willis and us. Before long, we found out how he was able to do it.

Mom didn't give any details as to how Willie got the money, but I thought that interviewing him would reveal it. The interview would also let me know his feelings and perceptions of growing up in Coulton. I decided Willie would be my next interviewee.

Mom continued telling her story.

In 2008, a recession struck the entire nation, and Coulton was no exception. The mines produced less coal, welfare benefits were cut, crime increased, drug abuse spread, and programs to help the poor decreased or were eliminated. It was a rough time for the nation, Appalachia, and Coulton.

Tim had been laid off, but fortunately I still had my post office job, so we were able to manage better than most. It took a few years before there was some improvement.

A concern that all coal families fear is injury or death in a mine accident or getting black lung disease. Your daddy followed in the footsteps of his daddy, and I always assumed that Willie would do the same. There were times when I thought about leaving Coulton and moving to a big northern city for a better life, but the thought was fleeting because injury and death were inevitable no matter where you worked or lived.

Mom had pretty much said all she wanted to say, and we agreed that her interview was finished. She had offered a lot of information that I thought was pertinent to my article and would be revealing to the readers.

Saturday was New Year's Eve, and I was excited that Bobbie Joe was coming over. I hoped we would spend the evening together and celebrate the new year with the townspeople.

Bobbie Joe arrived at the house right on time. For some reason, he didn't look like the same old guy I had known for more than fifteen years. Maybe it was the outfit he was wearing, his combed-back jet-black hair, his six-foot height, or his muscular build. I decided it was his cologne. We sat in the living room, and he handed me a white business envelope. I couldn't imagine what was in it. It was unsealed, and I took out its contents—a trifold sheet of paper. I opened it and read the first line.

"Mr. O'Mally, the University of Kentucky administration and faculty are pleased to inform you that you have been conditionally accepted into the mechanical engineering program for the Spring 2024 session."

The letter described the conditions, procedures, and process for registration. The final sentence expressed that he would be unable to secure a dorm room and that food and housing were up to him. I looked at Bobbie Joe and saw a huge smile on his face. I gave him a big hug and a sincere kiss.

"Congratulations," I said.

"Thank you," he replied.

I picked up a small box from the end table. It was wrapped with Christmas paper and tied with a red bow. I gave it to him.

Bobbie Joe opened the box and took out a key. "What's this for?" he asked.

"I know that it might be a while before you find housing, so I would like you to use my apartment until you do. I have two bedrooms, and I'm sure we can manage together until you find an apartment."

He thanked me and said that gave him one less thing to worry about. We spent the rest of the evening talking about Granny and other family members.

At ten o'clock, we walked to town to join the New Year's celebration. The ball at the top of the courthouse bell tower was lowered to a descending ten count, and horns and sirens welcomed the new year. I gave Mom a hug and Bobbie Joe a big kiss. I looked forward to all that the new year offered.

CHAPTER 11
MO'S STORY

Just like everyone in the family, I started grade school when I was five years old. The new county elementary school was no longer new. It had been open for more than fifteen years, and our entire family went there. School was easy for me, and I was often bored. I was an avid reader, and the first-grade teacher kept giving me books to read after I finished my classwork. I was an inquisitive child and would ask my parents all kinds of questions about the town, its people, and stories I had heard about mountain people. Why did we live in Coulton? What was life like beyond the mountains? What if I decided not to live in Coulton when I got older? They did their best to answer all my questions, but their answers always left me looking for more information. It was the same in school. I asked the teachers questions but never got the answers I was looking for. So, I finally decided I would find the answers to my questions on my own.

I met Sally Mae in first grade, and we are best friends to this day. I noticed Bobbie Joe on the first day of school. He was quiet and kept to himself. I always thought he was a deep thinker, and that was revealed as truth when he told his story. The three of us palled around through grade school. We enjoyed being with each other—we fished, told stories, and played games. We especially liked the town celebrations, the music, and the dancing. We didn't know much about life other than what happened in our families. I guess you could say we were oblivious to anything that happened on the other side of the mountain. My childhood was special, and I recalled all kinds of things that I would cherish forever.

In 2021, reality struck. Daddy had been sick for a while, and the heart condition he inherited caught up with him. He was working in the mine and collapsed one day. The ambulance took him to a Lexington hospital, and Mom and the rest of the family found out that he'd had a heart attack and would need a heart transplant. Mom put his name on the donor list, but he died before a compatible heart was found. We were devastated, the community mourned, and the mine company sent their condolences. Most of the village went to Daddy's funeral and burial. There was no celebration without Daddy. What would I do without him?

When I reached junior high, a door opened that I often wished had stayed closed. I learned how Coulton and our way of life was perceived by outsiders. I realized that I had led a sheltered life and that Dad and Mom had protected me from reality. Stories about our lifestyle, perceptions about our work ethic and behavior, and negative opinions about poor genetic makeup were revealed to me. When I first learned about these outsider views, I was shocked. The shock then turned to anger. I decided I would do my best when I got older to dispel the attitudes and perceptions outsiders had about our culture. I didn't know how, but I was determined to do it.

I found out that I had been insulated, and my friends and classmates knew way more than I did. I recalled Great-Granny's story as told by Granny. Her life in Scotland and Coulton. Her diaries revealed a lot about the cultural differences among the poor whites, Black people, and the rich when she first arrived in Coulton. She wrote about the mine company's control and the struggles she had with Great-Granddaddy. Much of what Granny had said wasn't written in the diaries and didn't give a true picture of how outsiders perceived mountain people. The true perception of how outsiders felt about us wasn't fully exposed until poverty became an embarrassing issue to the state and country. I left junior high knowing the true story.

In high school, I had no interest in sports or other activities. Sally Mae, Bobbie Joe, and I remained good friends. Neither one of them talked about how they felt about growing up in Coulton or what they knew about outsider perceptions. In my sophomore year, I joined the yearbook and newsletter clubs. That was when I realized I had an interest in journalism. I wrote the editorial for the school paper, which often got me in trouble. I had an uncanny desire to be truthful. I wrote articles about racism, discrimination, gays and lesbians, and women's rights. I was called into the principal's office many times and was told that Coulton was a conservative town and the topics I wrote about were not acceptable. Mom was called each time, and she tried to defend me. The outcome was that the controversial articles were never printed, and I had to wait until I graduated from high school to share my true feelings and opinions about America's cultural mores. I struggled through high school and bit my tongue often.

When I applied to Morehead State University, the journalism department asked for samples of my work. I sent them a few articles about American social issues and was accepted with merit and awarded a four-year scholarship. I had no idea that Morehead and the journalism department were liberal. They were both in for an awakening. I graduated from high school with honors and a couple of asterisks—watch out for her . . . she could be trouble . . . look out world. I worked in the town bakery during the summer and could hardly wait to get to college.

That summer, the Coulton mine went bankrupt, and all the miners lost their jobs. The miners protested and picketed outside the mine for back pay. There were no unions anymore, so they were on their own. A local lawyer represented the miners in court, and after four months, they won their back pay. Many of the miners left Coulton, some took up farming, others joined local miners who had struck small veins, and some took jobs in retail stores that had been built miles away from Coulton. When the dust settled, Coulton had lost nearly twenty families, and the population fell below six hundred. It was a rough time for many. Government benefits like food stamps and Medicaid became the only source of income. Poverty was everywhere. I left Coulton depressed and hoped my spirits would be lifted when I got to Morehead.

Willie, Mom, and I drove to my new home in the freshman dormitory. I was anxious to see what college had to offer. My roommate was from Lexington, and her family owned a horse farm. I could tell right away that we were different. The clothes that hung in her closet weren't handmade or bought from a thrift store. She had eight pairs of shoes lined up on the floor that were arranged in a seasonal order. I unpacked and hung my jeans and shirts—in no particular order. I took off my cowboy boots, changed into my tennis sneakers, and set my Sunday best shoes on the floor. Then I unpacked the rest of my things and rested on the bed. A half hour later, the door opened, and my roommate entered. She was short, had pink hair, was dressed in a bright-colored outfit, wore black high-top sneakers, had two piercings on each ear, arm tattoos, and three necklaces around her neck. My first thought was that Morehead was still living in the seventies. She introduced herself as Freebee, but her name was Mary. She smiled warmly and began to rattle off a whole bunch of things about her family and why she was at Morehead. She said her parents were wealthy and conservative and were embarrassed by her lifestyle. They wanted to hide her from their friends, so they sent her to Morehead. I wasn't sure about much of what Freebee said, but I was fairly sure we would get along.

I told her a little bit about Coulton and my family and said I was a journalism major and extremely liberal.

"I think we will turn out to be good friends," she said. I agreed.

We registered and started our classes. We were in an English class together, but because Freebee was an art major, we had different courses. I met my best college friend, Jenny, in my Introduction to Journalism class. She and I remained friends through the four years and would get together once in a while.

I met the chair of the journalism department on the second day. Ms. Dawson invited me to her office to talk about the direction I wanted to take while there. I told her I was passionate about women's rights, racial inequality, and class distribution of wealth. She suspected I would have interests in those areas because of the articles I had submitted for acceptance. She said they were the reason I was given a scholarship. Our first meeting went well, as did future meetings and the activities we participated in together.

My first article published in the Morehead student newspaper dealt with cafeteria food. I had learned that many students complained about the nutritional value of the meals served. Meals were loaded with carbohydrates and sugar. I interviewed students and cafeteria personnel to learn more about the students' concerns. After three meetings, students and the cafeteria director agreed to modify the menu and offer more balanced nutritional options. I was pleased with the outcome but never thought my first article would solve a cafeteria food problem. I hoped that my next article would be more substantive.

All went well for the rest of the year. I went home for holidays and breaks and returned to the Coulton bakery for the summer. I had applied for a newspaper internship but didn't get it. After I was home for a couple of days, I felt that something was wrong. Coulton just wasn't the same. I couldn't put my finger on it right away until I realized that the population decrease, the closure of the coal mine, and the high rate of poverty were the culprits. The stream of steady customers no longer existed, the town sidewalks and streets were vacant, and the town morale was poor. I struggled through the summer, bored and concerned that Coulton would become a ghost town like so many other Appalachian coal towns.

I returned to Morehead, ready to begin my second year. Everything started out well. My classes were going great, and I had written two meaningful articles for the newspaper.

In 2020, Biden took office despite Trump's accusation of a rigged election. Trump protested the results for the entire year, and on January 6, 2021, his followers stormed the Capitol in DC, causing deaths, injuries, and destruction. Accusations that there was voter fraud and miscalculations were rampant. The threat to fair and unbiased elections led to challenging democracy.

I was deeply concerned about voter rights and a fair election process, but I didn't want to get involved in politics, so I refrained from writing about the situation. I was more concerned with the election results and how it would affect women's rights, gun control, immigration, and diversity. I chose to write articles on abortion, contraception, and privacy and use social media as a platform. The articles in the school newspaper were well-received, and social media followers supported my views.

During the second semester of 2020, the first instances of the coronavirus were reported in the US. Initially, there was no outbreak on campus, but the administration was concerned. The school year ended in May, and I went back to Coulton for the summer. The bakery had closed, the streets and sidewalks were still vacant, and town morale was lower than it was the previous summer.

Mom and the rest of the family had a positive outlook despite the trying times. She worked at the post office, and Willie and Paul managed their hemp and cattle farm. Katy was in NYC, working in the fashion industry. John had left Coulton and was working in a Cleveland steel plant. I needed a job for the summer, and Mom was able to get me a summer job with the post office sorting mail and packages. The work was boring and slow. COVID hadn't hit Coulton yet, but the townspeople were worried. The virus was all that was needed to add to the town's woes.

I ended my summer job and went back to Morehead for my third year. A bunch of restrictions had been put in place because of COVID. We couldn't attend classes, and lectures were given remotely. College life had taken a hard turn. Socializing was key to a good college experience, and it was even worse for me because I couldn't conduct interviews in person and had to use social media to get information to write articles. I set up Facebook, Twitter, and Instagram accounts. I didn't mind using that approach, but my biggest concern was how to attract followers. I decided to use the journalism department database for contacts. I sent a Facebook message expressing my interest in abortion rights, gay relationships, and racism and discrimination and received thirty responses immediately. Within a few hours, I had over one hundred followers—and growing. I used Twitter and Instagram the same way and was surprised by the response and encouragement. I had created an audience to whom I could voice my beliefs and opinions and also avenues for others to express their points of view.

There were a number of rallies and protests scheduled on college campuses around the country for like-minded individuals and groups to express their views on social issues, but because of COVID, they were canceled. I felt that the best way to voice one's beliefs was through demonstrations and protests, but because students were unable to gather in groups on campus, social media became the medium of choice. I spent the rest of the semester organizing groups, writing a couple of articles for the university newspaper, and completing the requirements for a journalism degree next year.

Mom, Willie's family, and Paul all got COVID before I arrived for summer break. Their bouts weren't serious, and with medication, they were able to continue their regular routines after their illnesses. A number of townspeople caught COVID but survived. A few families with elders were less fortunate. The disease claimed thirteen people over seventy-five and a few who were younger. In total, there were twenty-seven deaths due to COVID. I didn't find any work in Coulton for the summer and ended up going back to Morehead to take a couple of classes so I could graduate early. The plan worked out, and I graduated magna cum laude after the first semester.

While I was completing my coursework, I wrote three articles about social issues. My adviser, Ms. Dawson, told me about a job opening with the *Lexington Gazette*. I applied and had an interview with the chief editor, Ben Williams. I submitted two of my articles with my resume and waited for an interview. It came three weeks after I applied for the position. We met again, and I was given a job offer.

I started my job at the *Gazette* on February 2, 2022. Just as I arrived, Ben called me into his office and said that the newspaper had received numerous calls about a plumbing problem in a Lexington Housing Project. He asked me to investigate the problem and see if it was newsworthy. I got hold of Pete, our photographer, and we drove to the apartment complex. The building was totally run-down on the outside and likewise on the inside. We approached a group of teens outside the main entrance, explained who we were, and said that a Mrs. Barren had contacted the newspaper to report a plumbing problem.

"Old Mrs. B is at it again," said one of the boys.

"She's in apartment 701," said another boy.

The elevator didn't work, so we had to climb seven flights of stairs. I got to the seventh floor, out of breath, and knocked on the door to apartment 701. Mrs. Barren answered and invited us in.

"Thank you for coming. I've been trying to get the landlord to do something about my broken toilet for two weeks. I didn't know what else to do, so I called the newspaper," she explained.

We listened and said that we would try to help. She showed us the bathroom. It was disgusting.

"How about a newspaper article about the bad plumbing conditions in this whole building," she said.

"I'll talk to the editor and see what we can do," I said.

Pete took a few pictures before we left.

When I got back to the office, I shared my experience with Ben. "What are we going to do about Mrs. Barren's situation?" I asked.

"Nothing," he said. I was surprised by his comment, but he continued. "That apartment complex and others have been a thorn in the community's heel for years. We tried to help with articles and contacting the housing authority, but it fell on deaf ears. We gave up and hoped that someone would eventually do something about the neglect. No one has, and we've given up."

I left his office, sat at my desk, and thought about Mrs. Barren and the thousands of others in the same predicament. I thought about Coulton and the years of outdoor plumbing and the polluted streams. The problem was different, but the outcome was the same. Not everything can be fixed. Battles needed to be chosen carefully and then followed through with conviction. I learned something from the investigation, and maybe that was Ben's intent. You win some, and you lose some!

After the plumbing assignment, Ben gave me assignments that were more to my liking. Each had substance and matched my beliefs. I investigated and wrote articles about poverty, women's reproductive rights, abortion, gun violence, mass murders, and class inequality and inequity.

I chose to tackle housing from a social class perspective, thinking back to Great Granny's first view of Coulton in 1925. While still sitting on the Greyhound bus, she immediately saw a distinct housing separation. Poor whites living in run-down houses on the "left" side of the valley, Black people living in shacks wedged in the middle, and the rich living in well-kept homes on the "right" side of the mountain. The scene and its reality created a lasting impression on her, one that she frequently questioned because she had never experienced such class distinction in Scotland.

I decided to investigate the housing system in Lexington. I read articles, newspapers, and books and learned that there were at least three different economic classes, each living separately from each other. Pete and I drove to each section and found housing patterns that were similar to Great-Granny's description of Coulton. Poor whites lived in housing projects and on city streets. There were run-down and neglected vacant houses with broken windows, yards overrun with weeds, and downed trees. We didn't see people on the sidewalks or on front porches. The streets were lined with broken-down cars and trucks. The only living inhabitants were feral cats and unleashed dogs. Pete took pictures, and we took off to another city neighborhood.

Most of the people in this part of the city were Black. There were rows and rows of high-rise tenement apartments and projects. Their appearance was similar to the houses and projects on the city streets we had just left. Groups of teens congregated in front of the buildings and houses and eyed us as we drove by. We didn't stop or take pictures.

Next, we drove to a suburban neighborhood just outside the city. Rows of houses lined the street. They were all similar in construction and well-maintained. The yards were clean, the lawns were cut, and children were everywhere. The scene looked like a '50s TV program.

Our next stop was a neighborhood with million-dollar homes. Everything was perfect . . . houses, yards, sidewalks, streets, and landscape. The people were the only things missing. We suspected that because it was a beautiful day, there was no need to venture outside.

We completed our tour with a drive through horse country. We saw acres of farmland, huge houses with black four-tier fencing surrounding them, horses running about, and impeccable landscaping. It was a class all to itself.

When we got back to the newspaper office, we spent a lot of time talking about the different lifestyles. Pete and I agreed that what we had seen was probably no different from other cities across the county. Of course, horse country set the area apart from others.

My investigation led to writing about the class system and lifestyles in America. I used Lexington as an example but realized a more comprehensive investigation should be carried out if I wanted to generalize it to a larger geographic area. I made sure that the article did not single out Lexington in a negative way. I completed the article and submitted it to Ben for approval. He advised me that once I started writing controversial articles, I would have to live with both positive and negative outcomes. I listened to his advice and had the article printed in the Saturday Review section of the *Gazette*. I had accepted that if I wanted to be a good investigative reporter, I would have to live with the fact that some readers would appreciate an informative article and others wouldn't.

When the article was printed, my social media followers made comments—nothing new, similar to most large cities, the haves and the have-nots, the American caste system prevails. Because the article was an informative piece, I had no intention of trying to change a structure that had probably existed since the beginning of time. I was pleased with the social media, message, and email formats that readers used for their responses and was confident that the approach would prove to be successful in the future.

There were so many hot topics to write about—Roe vs. Wade, women's reproductive rights, voting rights, COVID ending May 2023, class inequality and inequity, poverty, drugs, gun violence, school shootings, mass murders, immigration, and more. It was hard to decide which topics would interest readers and which would interest me. I decided that all my articles would be investigative and informative. I was not going to become a crusader to cure the social evils of America. My intention was to get readers thinking—but they could choose what to do about it.

One of my first articles was about women's reproductive rights. The issue had become extremely controversial since the Supreme Court struck down the 1973 Roe versus Wade abortion law on June 22, 2022. It overturned the rights of women to have an abortion, placing the decision in the hands of the states. The reaction was immediate. There were protests and demonstrations in every state.

My research revealed that the issue was not singular and limited to abortion. Women's reproductive rights were expanded to include prenatal care, safe childbirth, access to contraceptives, and access to legal and safe abortions. The entire controversy boiled down to a woman's right to choose. I had to be careful to remain objective when I wrote the article.

Again, my intent was to inform the public and not take sides. I continually reminded myself that I was reporting my findings, and it was up to my readers to decide on the action needed.

I finished the article and forwarded it to Ben for approval, and it was printed in the *Gazette's* Saturday edition. I continued to take on other issues for the rest of the year.

The feedback I got from readers was positive, mainly because I remained objective and neutral. I didn't commit to an issue one way or another, regardless of how I felt about it. The number of social media followers increased significantly from article to article, as did messages and emails. Many of the responses were from repeat readers. I felt as if I was getting the message out and contributing to worthwhile causes.

Ben recognized my popularity and asked me to write an article about Coulton. He hoped that circulation would improve and the newspaper would have more solid footing. In the middle of November 2023, I returned home and started writing my article series—*Coal Town Stories - 1925 to 2024.*

In writing my story about Appalachia, and specifically Coulton, I used the same approach that had worked with my university and newspaper articles. I conducted a series of interviews with family members and friends to obtain their personal feelings about living in a small coal town. I decided to interview my brother Willie first. He had been born and raised in Coulton and had never left. If anyone knew the real Coulton, he did.

CHAPTER 12
WILLIE'S STORY

I SAW WILLIE AND HIS FAMILY at the New Year celebration and reminded him about our interview. I was interested in how he perceived his life growing up in Coulton, why he didn't leave, and a passing comment Mom made about a legal incident he had been involved in. He was thirteen years older than me and had established a successful middle-class lifestyle.

Willie and I agreed to meet at the tavern at seven o'clock. I arrived early and sipped on a beer while I waited for him. He strolled in a half hour late with a huge smile on his face.

"Need another one?" he asked. He turned and walked to the bar, greeting his friends along the way. Willie was extremely popular.

He returned fifteen minutes later with two Bud Lights. He handed me a beer as he waved to another friend. "What's this interview about?" he asked.

"I'm writing an article for the *Gazette* about Coulton and its coal history," I said.

"What's that got to do with me?" he asked.

"I thought your story would make a great contribution."

"I'd love to help you, but I have one question. Do you want the true story or the made-up one?"

"The real story."

"Do you want to start now?" he asked.

"Now's good for me," I said.

"I haven't totally enjoyed my life here, and you know how I feel about the coal mining."

"That's exactly what I want to interview you about."

"Okay, let's get started," he said.

"Can you start with your first memory about our family or the town?"

My first recollection of Coulton and the coal mine was the time Daddy came home from the mine completely exhausted and covered with coal dust. He sat down on the floor and fell asleep. I was five years old and hadn't started school yet. That scene stuck in my mind for a long time.

When I got older, I was convinced I would never work in the mine. It wasn't the life I wanted for my family or me. I promised myself that I wouldn't go down that road, and I didn't. I remember starting school. The old one-room schoolhouse had burned down long ago, but it didn't matter because the new county elementary school had opened. There were plenty of stories about how the schoolhouse caught fire, but there were just a couple of my friends who really knew what happened. I wonder if the police ever found out who burned the schoolhouse down.

I had lots of friends at home and at school. We did the regular things that young boys do. We got into trouble once and awhile but nothing serious. We played lots of baseball in the summer and goofed around in the winter. I liked school and was good at math. I didn't care about reading so much. It was difficult for me. I remember that reading, writing, and spelling were my worst nightmares. The school tested me and said I had dyslexia. I was given special help and was able to learn how to live with the disability, but it was hard on me. Some of the kids made fun of me because I couldn't read well, and they called me Tard. That name stuck with me all through grade school, and there were some days I didn't want to go to school. Mama was sensitive to my feelings but made me go to school anyway. When I was in third grade, I got into my first fight because of my learning problem. Jake made fun of me all the time. I put up with it for a few years until I couldn't take his name-calling anymore. We had gone outside after lunch, and he started in on me. All the kids had surrounded us, and I threw the first punch. Blood poured out of his nose, and he ran into the school. It wasn't much of a fight because there was only one punch, and it was a winner. From that day on, things got better, and no one made fun of me or called me Tard.

My early school years went by fast, and I started junior high when I was eleven. I liked it a lot because we didn't have to read aloud, there were shop classes, and I played on the baseball team. I was a pitcher and a good hitter. Playing baseball gave me a lot of confidence even though I continued to struggle with reading. I knew that whatever I did with my life, it would not be coal mining. I liked auto mechanics a lot because it was hands-on and didn't require a lot of reading. I thought it might be an excellent job after high school. I remember the first time I realized I liked girls. I met Mary Beth. I never really talked to her, but I knew I liked her.

The two junior high years went by quickly, and in high school I realized that I would need to decide about work when I graduate. I continued to learn more about auto mechanics and thought it would be a good way to earn a living. The guidance counselor suggested I go to a community college in Richmond to learn more. I had no interest in leaving Coulton, and Mary Beth and I had become sweethearts. I chose to stay at home and got a job at Rudi's Auto when I graduated. Mary Beth and I continued to date, and we talked about getting married.

At the end of my senior year, I found out that Mr. Willis was selling his five-acre farm, and I talked to him about selling it to me. Of course, I didn't have a penny to my name. He agreed to sell the farm with a deposit. That's when Daddy and Mama said they would loan me five thousand dollars. They questioned that I knew nothing about farming, but I told them Mr. Willis agreed to teach me. My auto mechanic classes in high school prepared me for the mechanical work, and Mr. Willis showed me how to grow tobacco and raise cows. I started out with three acres of tobacco, one bull, and three heifers.

The first couple of years were hard. We had a drought, and I lost all my tobacco seedlings to bad weather. My bull died, and I was unable to get more cows. I was totally frustrated and began thinking I made a huge mistake. I still owed Mr. Willis and Daddy and Mama thousands of dollars. I wanted to get married to Mary Beth, but there was no way. I was broke. I had heard stories about farmers making a lot of money by growing marijuana. It was illegal, but it still grew on lots of county farms. I talked to a few people about who I could contact and learned about the Cornbread Mafia.

In 1989, a group of Appalachian men started the largest domestic marijuana distribution network in US history. I had no way of contacting the leaders and wasn't sure I should. If I ever got caught growing illegal weed, I would end up in jail, to say nothing about how angry and embarrassed Daddy and Mama would be, and my future with Mary Beth would likely fall apart. But I was in such debt that I had no other option. I found out who the contact was and made a deal to grow three acres of weed the first year. All worked out well, and I made a little money. Certainly not enough to pay off Mr. Willis and Daddy and Mama though. I needed more land. I took the profits I made the first year and bought five more acres.

The following year, I grew eight acres of weed and made enough money to pay off my debts. Paul had graduated from high school and joined me in my illegal venture. I worried every day that we would get caught and end up in jail. Five years passed, and we bought ten more acres and continued to grow. There were a number of farmers who had resorted to growing for the Mafia. The law had turned its head, and the farmers were left alone. I suspected the Mafia had taken care of that.

Mary Beth and I had been married for three years and had two children. We had bought a ten-acre farm outside of Coulton and raised cattle and grew tobacco. Mary Beth, Daddy, and Mama never knew about the weed business until the sheriff's department raided our barns. Paul and I had kept raising weed on the first farm. One day, we had just finished hanging the weed to dry and a bunch of sirens and police cars pulled up *in front of the barn. We looked at each other and ran back to the barn. We flew out the back door and headed for the woods. As I ran, I knew there was no way we were getting out of this. Unfortunately, Paul tripped over a log and fell to the ground in pain. I knelt to help him, and the cops were right on us. We were cuffed, Paul was helped up, and we were put in jail. My biggest fear had turned to reality. We were in jail for a couple of days till Daddy bailed us out. A court date was set, and I was fined ten thousand dollars. It could have been worse, but I had a good lawyer, and Daddy knew the right people. I had the money and was able to return home. When I opened the front door, I felt something was wrong. I called for Mary Beth, but she was gone. I didn't blame her for leaving and taking the kids. Who would want to be married to an outlaw? We got together over the next couple of months and patched things up. I promised I would not go down the weed path again.*

Paul and his wife got a divorce. We started growing hemp, which was legal. A new crop had come to Kentucky. Well, it wasn't new because back in the 30's Kentucky led the country in hemp production. In a few years, I was able to work with the state and became a certified hemp grower. My illegal endeavor followed me for years, but I was eventually able to put it in the back of my mind. Mama and Daddy were good to me, but I knew what I had done embarrassed them and the rest of the family.

For the longest time, when I walked down the street or went to church, I felt all eyes were on me. Mary Beth and her family were shamed and still feel it to this day. My biggest concern was our three children. They had to deal with negative comments from their friends that I was a jailbird.

Willie stopped and looked at me. "I hope my past hasn't affected you while you were growing up and even now," he said.

"I know that was a difficult story to tell. One that I had heard pieces of over the years. Your past had no effect on me at all. Thanks for sharing your story with me. I have another question. How was it growing up in Coulton knowing its history and generations of poverty?"

"I think that's why I made that wrong decision when I graduated from high school. I didn't want to grow up a coal miner and be owned by the company. It just wasn't me. I wanted my own life and money."

As far as Coulton's history and the stories that have been told about hillbillies and rednecks, I learned a long time ago that most of the stories aren't true. Growing up here wasn't at all what was portrayed by outsiders. Sure, we like our isolation and our way of doing things, but that doesn't mean we're ignorant, backward, lazy, and live off government programs. I recognize that poverty has always been with us, but we have learned to live with it and still have a strong, positive culture. Practically every person in this town would bend over backwards to help one another. Despite the negative outsider stories, we are hardworking, honest, and God-fearing.

As far as stories about growing weed and making moonshine, I was one of the few that went down that path, and I will regret it for the rest of my life. Stories about family feuds, drunken brawls, and incest are made up to attract visitors to see the animals in the Coulton cage. No one seems to talk or write about our family traditions like holiday and family celebrations, our love for folk music and clog dancing, the hundreds of villagers that fought in the wars, and the successful men and women who have contributed to making Coulton and our country great.

Willie finished, and I felt like he had captured my feelings and the community's sentiments exactly. I was so proud of him. I thanked him and gave him a big hug. He had been talking for almost two hours, and the band started setting up to play. Ironically, the name of the band was "The Rednecks." I laughed and thought that maybe the negative could be positive after all.

Before I began a series of interviews with the townspeople, I checked in with Ben, Bobbie Joe, and Sally Mae.

I messaged Ben and asked if he had published the promo for the coal town article and if he'd received any feedback. He messaged back and said the promo was published last Saturday, but there was very little response. He said he would publish it again and let me know the outcome. It was January 4, and I had planned to finish the article by January 15 and then return to Lexington. I felt that I was on schedule and planned to have the remaining interviews completed in a week.

I called Bobbie Joe to see how he was doing. He seemed in good spirits. "All well here," he said. "I found a job and start classes in two weeks. I've been looking for an apartment that's in my budget but haven't found anything yet. When are you coming back to Lexington?"

"I should finish here by mid-January. I'll let you know exactly when by the end of the week. By the way, make sure you clean your messes up. I don't want to come home and find my apartment a wreck," I said.

"Not to worry. I've been cleaning up after every party so far," he replied. He ended the comment with a snicker, and I said goodbye.

Next, I gave Sally Mae a call, but she didn't answer. I left a message asking how she was doing. She had returned to her accountant job just after Christmas, and I hadn't spoken to her since then. I was sure she was busy and enjoying her job and social life. I decided rather than wait for a return call, I would drive to Richmond. I needed computer ink anyway.

I got to her apartment near seven o'clock. She was completely surprised and greeted me with a huge hug. We settled in and talked about family for a while.

"You hungry?" she asked.

"Starving," I said.

"Would you like to fix something here or go out?"

Richmond was a college town with plenty of bars and music, so I said, "Let's go out. I need a beer and a burger."

We chose to go to the Spur, which was a popular country bar where most of the EKU students spent time together. It was Wednesday, and I wasn't sure there would be music, but we found a booth next to the dance floor so we could get to the bar if it got crowded. We ordered our food and drinks and waited to see if a band arrived.

It was just like old times. We talked about our work and futures. We brought up memories of old boyfriends, which reminded me of Bobbie Joe staying in my apartment. Sally Mae knew nothing about the arrangement, and I didn't mention it.

I had just taken a bite of my burger when two boys approached our booth. I hadn't been in this scene for a while and wondered how it would go. It was always intriguing to see what their first moves would be.

The taller blond boy started. "Are you two ladies southern belles or hillbillies?" he asked. That was the wrong first move for both of us. We ignored them, and they walked away.

The band began to set up, and we were the first to hit the dance floor. During the second song, two guys cut in and asked us to dance. It was a slow song, so we decided to sit it out. We walked back to our booth, and they followed. I was curious about how they would approach us.

The dark-haired, brown-skinned boy stared at me. "Do you mind if we join you?" he asked.

I looked at Sally Mae, and she nodded okay, so I said, "Sure, as long as you don't start the conversation by asking if we're southern belles or hillbillies."

He had a confused look on his face for a few seconds but then asked if we were EKU students. I was flattered because I had been out of college for two years and thought the aging process had already taken hold of me.

"No, we're childhood friends, and I'm just visiting," I said.

Sally Mae jumped in. "Where are you guys from? I detect a northern accent."

"Jersey," they both said simultaneously.

"What brings you to Kentucky?" I asked.

"We're freshmen and going to school here.

"Why did you choose EKU?" asked Sally Mae.

"Lots of guys from Jersey go to school here because tuition and room and board are more reasonable, and you get a good education."

"What are your majors?" I asked.

"We're both majoring in criminal justice and hope to get into law enforcement when we graduate," the taller of the two said.

"Did you guys go to college?" the other guy asked.

"Yeah, we both graduated four years ago. I majored in accounting and have a job here," said Sally Mae.

The other brother looked at me. "How about you?" he asked.

"I went to Morehead, majored in journalism, and work as a reporter for the *Lexington Gazette*," I said.

I began to sense that the boys were legitimately okay and not necessarily interested in a pickup. I liked the fact that they were from the north—an interview with two "outsiders" would complement the article.

We introduced ourselves to each other. The taller of the two was named Angelo, and the other Dominic.

"My name is Mo, and my best friend is Sally Mae," I said. "I grew up in a small coal town in Appalachia, and Sally Mae moved to the town when she was six. We've been best friends since. I'm working on a newspaper project and interviewing people to build the content. Would the two of you be receptive to answering a few questions?"

They looked at each other and nodded.

"That's great! First question," I said. "When you decided to go to school in the South, what was your first thought about the culture?" I asked.

Angelo responded first.

Well, we were born and raised in Jersey and had never been to the south but heard plenty of stories. Some Northerners talk about how poor people are and how most have no education. They say that they're overly dependent on government programs. All of these contribute to a negative opinion. There's another school of thought that says the women run around barefoot and pregnant, incest is widespread, and the children are illegitimate, which leads to people calling you hillbillies and white trash.

Dominic chimed in.

On the other side of the coin, Southerners believe that Northerners are mostly Italians, belong to the Mafia, and are all born in New York state. The name given to us during the Civil War was "Yankees," and it's still used today. As you can see, our interpretations are different, but both are negative. We just use different names to describe each other.

I looked at Sally Mae to see if I could read her reaction to what we had just heard. I didn't look very long before she asked, "What are your parents' backgrounds?"

Dominic answered that question.

Our grandparents came from Naples, Italy in the late 1800s. They settled in New York and later moved to Jersey. My grandpa laid blacktop streets, and my grandma raised seven children. My father works in a steel plant, and my mother works as a waitress. Both my grandparents and parents have worked hard their whole lives. Their strong work ethic was handed to my brother, me, and our other siblings. We know the value of a dollar and spend it wisely. We were raised as Catholics and have strong values and morals. We are strong patriots, support our family, and help our neighbors in need.

I was surprised by his story and how closely it resembled mine. There were so many similarities between our families—migration to America, blue-collar jobs, patriotism, religion, and feelings about being poor and discriminated against. I realized that regardless of where you're from, north or south, misconceptions and false stories develop and are handed down through generations. It was almost eleven o'clock, and we had gone through a few beers and a lot of talk. I was so happy to have met the twins and recognized that their outsider story was a missing piece in my article.

We exchanged goodbyes, and then Sally Mae and I went back to her apartment. I left early the next morning. I was halfway home when I realized I had forgotten to buy computer ink. But that didn't matter anymore. I had gotten much more out of the trip than I could have imagined.

Next on my agenda was deciding who else I would interview. I had a long list of possibilities, but I wanted to find someone who knew the history of Coulton since its very first settlers. I knew I was asking for a lot, but knowing how it all began would add another missing link to the story.

I walked into the kitchen and saw Mom making supper. "Mom, do you know who the oldest person in Coulton is?" I asked.

"Well, Granny used to talk about a man named Isaac Williams. He lives up the hollow. His family is supposed to be the first settlers who came to Coulton. He'd be around a hundred years old—if he's still alive. Why don't you ask around town to see if he is and how you can find him," she said.

I walked out the front door and headed to the general store, where I found Mr. Gentry behind the counter, putting cans on a shelf. "Hi, Mr. Gentry, how are you?" I asked.

"Fine. How can I help you, Mo?" he asked.

"Do you know if Mr. Williams is still alive and living in the hollow?"

"He's alive. His daughter was in the other day buying food for him."

I rushed out of the store. I hadn't been up the hollow since Bobbie Joe and I went squirrel hunting when we were in junior high. I knew how to get there but wasn't sure where Mr. William's house was. I returned home, told Mama what I had learned, and planned to go up the hollow early in in the morning.

The following morning, I was up early and out the door. On the way, I met a woman and asked about Mr. William's house.

"It's the green house about a mile down, just past the church on the right," she said.

I found the house without any trouble. An old man sat on the porch, rocking in a chair and smoking a corncob pipe. I approached him and asked if he was Mr. Williams.

"Sure am. How can I help you, young lady?" he asked.

I introduced myself and told him I would like to interview him for an article I was writing about Coulton.

"I'd love to help, but my memory isn't as good as it used to be," he said.

"That's okay. We'll just go back as far as you can."

I realized that what he told me might be secondhand and maybe third, and that stories not told firsthand can change significantly when passed from person to person over time, but if any of it was even half true, I would be happy.

"Do you have time now?" I asked.

"Sure do. How fir back do you want me to go?"

"Start as far back as you can," I said.

I can tell you about when my great-granddaddy came to Kentucky and settled in Harlan County. It was about five year after the Civil War. I think it was 1871 when Harlan County was founded. My family lived in Mississippi, and we was cotton pickers. The story goes that after Lincoln freed the slaves, our family moved to Kentucky to cut and put up 'baccy.

I stopped for a minute because I was having a hard time understanding Mr. William's accent. It was something I had never heard before and seemed like a cross between old English and a strong southern dialect. I figured that the interview would take a longer time because I couldn't understand half of what he was saying. I had taken a phonetics class at Morehead and had a good understanding of the standard English dialect, but Mr. William's dialect was specific to a US region and population. His vocabulary, grammar, and phonology were distinctly different from my family's and most of Coulton's. I decided to interpret his accent as best as I could and follow up with translating it later. I figured I would need to research the history of regional dialects and their origin to fully comprehend the unusual dialect.

I apologized for the pause and asked him to continue.

My family first settled in Mississippi in the late 1700s. My great-granddaddy came over from England around then. We was slaved to a rich and powerful family. The story goes that we worked hard and did what we was told. Black people had no say, and you did what you had to do to live. One of Great-Granddaddy's children was born to the landowner, and I was part of him. Now his daughter moved to Kentucky and Harlan County, and that's where my family started, and Coulton is where we was raised.

Back in the 1700s, large sailing vessels called "frigates" or "schooners" came from Scotland. The trip was filled with hardships including cramped conditions, disease, poor food, and bad weather. Passengers slept on mattresses stuffed with straw or a pile of wood, and burlap bags was used for blankets. Men, women, and children were on the ships for weeks without good food or clean water, and they feared a shipwreck, death, sickness, and disease. The story that Daddy heard from his daddy and him from his daddy was that there was fifteen in our family who began the trip from Scotland to America and made it to the port in New York City.

From there it took a lot of time to get to Mississippi. There's no tellin' why they went there, but that's where they ended up. From what my daddy said, that's where there was work picking cotton. Our family grew to more than twenty, and after they was freed, they went to Kentucky to work in the back fields. When Harlan County was founded, my family moved to Coulton to continue farmin' and later worked in the coal mines. When my family first came to Colton, they decided to live in the hollow, and that's where we been ever since.

I think when I was about six, my daddy moved our family to the hollow and built a cabin, and that's where I now live. There was nine chillin in the family. They all died 'cept me. My wife, Betha, and me had seven chillin, and I lived past all of dem. When I was old enough, I worked the 'baccy and raised a few cows. I ain't never had much, includin' money, so I lived a poor life. I always said you don't really know what yer missin' when you don't have nuttin'.

I listened to Mr. Williams for more than an hour and asked if he would like to take a break. He said he'd like to get some water then got up from the rocking chair and walked into his house. He returned a few minutes later with two glasses of lemonade and handed one to me.

"Thought you might be a bit thirsty like me," he said.

I took a long gulp and then set the glass on the porch table. "Thank you. I really needed that," I said. "Could you tell me how it was for you when you were growing up in Coulton?"

Like I told you before, 'bout the first things I remember was when I was around six. I was the oldest of all of us chillin. My mama worked hard raisin' us and workin' in the fields. My sister Betha took care of me most until she was old enough to work the fields. I never had any schoolin' 'cept what Bertha taught me. I learned my numbers and could read a bit by the time I was ten. Then I went to the fields wit the rest of the family. I do member goin' to town a little bit when there was a party like the Ford of Jooly. I like the town, and the white peoples was good too.

I went to WWII wit my friend Eddy and fought on the front line in France. Eddie didn't come home with me. I still miss him today. After I got home, there was a big celebration in town for all the soldiers—black and white. There was a statue put up for us. That same night is when I met Bertha. She was from the hollow and wit her family. I never seen her before and was happy to meet her. We courted for a year or so and got married. We raised seven chillin' who all left Coulton after grade school to work in the big-city factories. They come by now and then, but mostly then. Bertha stayed wit me for sixty years and died ten year ago. I've been sittin' on this porch for all those years waitin' to join her.

I was captivated by Mr. William's story and anxious to learn more. I wanted to know his feelings about living in Coulton, so I asked, "How would you say your life has been being born and raised in Coulton your whole life?"

That's an easy question to answer. When you was poor your whole life and livin' wit families like your own, you don't know no different. I always wanted more for my family and even thought about movin' north a few times, but Betha would have none of that. I made enough money farmin' and workin' in the mine to feed my family and have a roof over our heads. I wouldn't say that I was jealous of the white and Black people who had money, better houses, or schoolin', but I wouldn't have minded it. It would have been a better life for my family. Even though we was poor, I worked hard, was honest, and always put our lives in the hands of the Lord. I guess you could say that Coulton was a good town to live in because we all got along and understood and accepted our lot.

I had one more question. "Can you tell me about working in the coal mine?" I asked.

When I got to be thirteen, my daddy told me dat it was time to work in the mine. He had been workin' there since he was twelve. I would see him come home after dark just as tired and dirty as could be. He coughed a lot and was spittin' up blood. Mammy took care of him, but it didn't help. He died when he was thirty-three and left Mammy with nine chillin'. I worked in the mine till I was twenty-three then quit. I hated it, and some of my friends and family was already sick. Me and Bertha rented a small piece of land and grew 'baccy and raised a few cows. We made enough money with Betha cleaning for the rich people to get by.

I thanked Mr. Williams for sharing his story from a three-generation perspective. He gave me more than I expected, and I felt it would contribute significantly to my article. I looked at my notes and realized I had a lot of research and translating to do. I had written everything phonetically and needed to make sense of it so the story could be understood by my readers.

When I got home, I found what I was looking for in Wikipedia. The article was titled *Older Southern American English* and is paraphrased as follows.

HISTORY

A diverse set of dialects was spoken widely in the southern US until the Civil War. Gradually transforming among white speakers at the turn of the twentieth century after the Depression, WWII, and the civil rights movement. By the mid-twentieth century, among white Southerners, these local dialects had consolidated into or been replaced by more regional unified Southern American English. Meanwhile, among Black Southerners, these dialects transformed into a fairly stable vernacular English now spoken among Black people. Certain features unique to older Southern US English persist today, though typically only among Black speakers or among very localized white speakers. Different American English dialects evolved two hundred years ago from English migrants who settled in Appalachia. The English spoken by the colonists was quite different from any variety of English spoken today.

ENGLISH LANGUAGE EVOLUTION

Modern English 1750 – 2024	Elizabethan English 1500 – 1750	Middle English 1300 - 1700	Old English 650 – 1300
poor	poor	poor let	earn
friend	friend	frend	frond
girl	girl	gerie	girdle
boy	boy	boy	boa
woman	woman	woman	woman
father	father	fader	feeder

In the 1600s, modern English and older Southern dialects originated in varying degrees from a mix of the speech of later immigrants from many different regions of the British Isles (Scotland) who moved to the American South in the seventeenth and eighteenth centuries as well as the English creole speech of African and African American slaves. Northern English and Southern backcountry settled in Appalachia and formed the Appalachian dialect. In 1860, many different Southern accents—called plantation accents—developed and were spoken by lower-class white and Black people. Today, the linguistic divide is largely between Black and white Southerners.

SOUTHERN DIALECTS

potato	oil	know
trader	all	knower
tomato	young	wash
madder	youngin	warsh
tobacco	mine	here
backer	your in	cheer
isn't	big	horse
hain't	begin	herse
grease	sitting	them
grease	sitting	dem

Source: Leon Swarts, Author

I completed my research on the evolution of the English language and Southern dialects and had a better understanding of the origin and history of the dialects spoken in the past and present. It was interesting and helped me interpret Mr. William's story. I also learned about the evolution of Southern vocabulary, grammar, vocabulary, and phonology and applied that to the notes I had taken during Mr. William's interview, writing the piece so that it was more in line with modern English.

CHAPTER 13
TOWN STORIES

I spent two days editing Mr. Williams's interview and left some of his everyday language in place. I wanted readers to hear his story in his exact words.

Having worked on that, I began thinking about who to interview next. I had the stories from my family, friends, and Mr. Williams edited and ready for print, but I wanted to find someone else with a story that would pique the readers' interest. I decided to interview an older woman and recalled Mom mentioning an older woman who had spent all her life in Coulton. She didn't know her name but heard that she was in the Harlan nursing home. I decided to make an early morning visit.

The drive was just six miles from Coulton, so I arrived early at nine o'clock. I approached the receptionist's desk and told her who I was. My next move was iffy because I knew that giving me a person's name would break confidentiality, but I decided to try anyway. Just as I was about to ask the receptionist, a spunky lady rolled up to the counter in a wheelchair. She was very friendly and asked my name and why I was there. I told her I was looking for a woman who had lived in Coulton her whole life and was now living there in the nursing home.

She looked straight at me. "That's me," she said.

I couldn't believe my luck to have stumbled upon her. The receptionist was just as surprised. "Mrs. Tilson, this is Mo Healy from the *Lexington Gazette*. She's interviewing people from Coulton for an article she's writing. If it's okay with you, she'd like to interview you," she explained.

"That's fine with me," Mrs. Tilson said.

"If you want, you can use the library. Mrs. Tilson knows where it is," the receptionist said.

When we got to the library, we sat in a far corner so we wouldn't bother anyone.

"Well, what would you like to know about Coulton and me?" she asked.

"When did your family come to Coulton? And how did they get here?" I asked.

My Ma came to Coulton when she was twenty-five years old and died ten years ago when she was eighty-nine. She told me stories about sailing on a ship with a group from her hometown in Scotland in the spring of 1925 and her travels to get to Coulton. It took more than ten days to get to the New York City port. She said the journey was hard with a lack of food and water, dirty sleeping conditions, disease, and fights. I remember one story she told me about a man from Scotland who was stabbed by another man for stealing his food. His wife was very young and pregnant. Ma said she took a liking to the girl because her husband was mean to her, so she helped her during the trip. When her husband got stabbed, he was bleeding all over the place. Ma had trained as a nurse back in Scotland, so she knew what to do. She saved the man's life. After they got off the ship, she never saw him again.

I was shocked by what she had just said. I was confident that Mrs. Tilson had described the same ship incident that Great-Granny had written about in her diary. I didn't know if I should tell Mrs. Tilson that my great-granddaddy was the man she saved. I did.

She continued to tell more stories about the journey on the ship.

When we arrived in New York, we found out that a lot of people from Scotland went on to live in Kentucky. They were able to find train and bus transportation all the way to Harlan County. There was twenty men and five women in our group. None of the men had ever worked in the coal mines, but there was a big need for miners, so they was all hired. The women, including me, didn't have many options. There weren't any jobs for women in the mine, so we stuck together until we found someone to marry. Within two years, we were all married. My husband and I settled in Coulton, and he worked in the mine. Before long, we had five children. We lived in company housing and lived paycheck to paycheck. We went through all the ups and downs just like everyone else who was a mining family. The strikes, deaths, injuries, layoffs, and promises for a better life that never happened. We was poor our whole lives, but there was a good thing about living in Coulton—the townspeople had developed a lifestyle and friendship that carried us through all the tough times. We were there to help one another and enjoy the good times and struggle through the bad times. When the kids got old enough, they left Coulton and now live and work in the big northern cities. There are so many stories I could tell you about my Ma and Pa and my husband and me that would keep you here for days, but I'm getting tired now and think I need a nap.

"Just one more question, if you don't mind," I said.

"Okay."

"What was it like growing up and becoming an adult in Coulton?"

Well, I can tell you there was some good and some bad. When I was little, I played around the house with my brothers and sisters. I didn't have no schoolin', so my readin' and numbers was never good. I was the oldest of seven brothers and sisters, so I went to work in the fields when I was ten. I hated farmin' and always dreamed of traveling. Even goin' Back to Scotland. But I never did. When I was fifteen, I met my husband. He worked in the Harlan mine. We married and had six chillins. We was poor, but we were able to survive. We stayed in Coulton our whole lives even though our kids all left when they was old enough. We liked Coulton because all the families got along, includin' the Black people and the rich. We had a lot of celebrations together. We liked country music and dancing. We was a churchgoing family and obeyed all the commandments.

I hoped Mrs. Tilson had the energy for one more question and didn't fall asleep before she could answer it. "One more thing . . . what can you tell me about the coal mine companies?" I asked.

They was the owners of everything . . . houses, stores, land, and the like. Once you worked for them, they owned you too. My husband hated the mine work but was stuck. Our kids saw it all and left as soon as they could. We was never paid enough for the hard work, and there was deaths and injuries all the time because there was no safety laws. But we had no other choice but to live here.

Mrs. Tilson and I had been talking for almost two hours, and I didn't want to push it. I got up and followed her to the hallway, where she gave me a big hug. "Good luck with your article," she said, "and I hope I was helpful."

I watched as she wheeled herself down the hallway. She reminded me so much of Granny, and I was surprised that their paths never crossed while they both lived in Coulton. For some reason, I wasn't sure that was true.

I walked past the receptionist's counter and thanked her for her help.

"How'd it go?" she asked.

"Well," I replied. I didn't want to share the unbelievable coincidence of Great-Granny and Great-Granddaddy being on the ship together and Mrs. Tilson's mother saving his life, but I could hardly wait to get home to tell Mom about it.

Mom was upstairs in her bedroom when I got home. "How was your trip to Harlan?" she asked.

"I learned something about your grandparents that you're not going to believe. Mrs. Tilson, the woman I interviewed at the nursing home, told me a story about her grandmother's voyage from Scotland in 1925."

"That's the same year Great-Granny came here," Mom said.

"That's only part of the story. Not only did she come to America the same year, but she was on the same ship. She told me all about the hardships on board and a specific story about a fight between two passengers. She was a nurse and saved one of the men's lives. His name was William Healy," I said excitedly.

Mom looked at me, startled.

"Did you or Granny know Mrs. Tilson?" I asked.

"No, we never met her. At least, I never met her. I don't know about Granny," she said.

"She said she never met Granny, which is surprising to me since practically everyone knows everyone in Coulton."

"Did you get her first name?" asked Mom.

"She never told me, but I heard the receptionist mention her name when she said goodbye to her. It was Frances, and she was named after her mother."

Mom's face reddened.

"What is it?" I asked.

"If I'm not mistaken, Granny mentioned that Great-Granny talked about a friend named Frances who helped her when she and Great-Granddaddy got into arguments. Granny didn't talk much about the woman, but for some reason, she played a big part in why your great-grandparent's marriage was so rocky," Mom said.

I didn't ask any more questions, deciding to let sleeping dogs lie.

I left Mom and went to my room to work on Mrs. Tilson's story. While doing so, I thought ahead to my next interview, thinking a young mother who wasn't born or raised in Coulton would be good. Maybe someone who had relocated here from the north could provide insight into why she and her family had moved to Coulton.

The next morning, I woke up late, had breakfast, and then took a walk along the creek. It was cold, and a late evening snowfall had left a few inches of snow on the ground. When I got to the bench that Bobbie Joe and I had sat on, I rested. I noticed groups of children sledding down a small hill that ended at the creek. They were laughing and screaming with delight. I had a flashback to when Sally Mae, Bobbie Joe, and I did the same thing.

The last group to come down the hill was a woman and two children. She was on her own sled, and the boys shared one. When they got to the bottom of the hill, her boys' sled kept sliding toward the creek. The water wasn't frozen over, and I knew the sled might end up in the water. It did, but the creek was only a couple of feet deep, and the boys were okay. The woman ran to them and helped them out of the water. I came over to give her a hand.

When we got to the bench, we all sat down. The woman pulled out a large thermos and four cups. She poured hot chocolate for the boys and offered me a cup. I was a bit chilled, so I gladly took it. She thanked me for helping and told me her name was Sharon McNaulty, and her children were Patrick and Shawn. She asked the boys if they were ready to go, and they started to walk toward the parking lot.

Before they reached their car, I hurried over and told her I was writing an article about Coulton, and if she had time, I'd like to interview her. She said she'd meet me at Cora's Diner at two o'clock.

"Will the boys be with you?" I asked.

"I'm going to get them into some dry clothes and drop them off at their friend's house, but I can bring them by after our interview if you'd like to talk to them," she said.

"That would be great. I'd like to ask them about their opinion of Coulton."

I arrived at the diner at two, and Sharon was sitting in a booth waiting for me. We greeted each other, and I gave her more details about my project.

"Okay, so what's your first question?" she asked.

"How did you end up in Coulton?"

It was accidental. My husband was offered a manager's job at a strip mall in Berea five years ago. We had no intention of leaving our home in Louisville, but the job offer was so good, and we wanted a change, so we accepted it. The boys were two years old, and it was a good time to move before they started school. We took a road trip to Berea before my husband started, and he loved it.

We continued our trip and drove into Coulton. We liked what we saw, talked to some of the townspeople, and checked out the housing situation. We recognized the three distinct housing sections immediately. Then we drove to a new subdivision a mile outside of Coulton and found our dream house. We hadn't looked for a house in Berea but felt that Coulton and the house we found were perfect for raising our boys. We bought the house, and Hank travels back and forth to Berea five times a week. He doesn't mind the drive and feels that it's better that he doesn't live in the same town as the store renters and workers. So far, everything's working out and we're happy.

"What do you like about Coulton?" I asked.

Before we moved here, we walked through town and talked with a lot of people. Everyone was so friendly, and that alone convinced us to settle in Coulton. During our walk, we stopped in a few stores and met the merchants. We asked them why they kept their businesses in Coulton instead of moving to more populated towns. The answer from all of them was the cultural cohesiveness among the townspeople that they had developed over generations. There was a willingness to help one another in times of need. I especially like the smallness. The streets weren't overrun with cars and trucks, and children played freely in their yards and on the streets. It was safe! We also learned about the holiday, wedding, and seasonal celebrations that are held in the community barn. Overall, Coulton seemed ideal for us. We haven't been disappointed one bit since we've been here the last four years.

As Sharon finished, the diner door swung open and two short-haired six-year-olds burst into the room. They ran to their mother, gave her a hug, and asked if they could have an ice cream cone.

"It's freezing outside, and you want ice cream?" she said. "First, I want you to meet Mo. She has some questions for you about living here."

The boys looked at me, and I realized they wanted the questions right away, so I asked, "Why do you like living here?"

Shawn was the first to respond. "I like it here because I have lots of friends and I can see them at school and when we're in town. I like playing baseball, and we have a good team. I'm the best pitcher and the best hitter."

"No, you're not," said Patrick.

"I'm better than you, right Mommy? I like it here because I have a girlfriend."

"No, you don't. She's *my* girlfriend."

"Mommy, can we get ice cream now?" Shawn asked.

At that point, I knew the interview with the boys was over. There was no way I was going to put myself in the middle of an argument between two six-year-olds.

Sharon looked at me with a shrug and said, "I think ice cream is more important than your questions."

"I agree," I replied and thanked her for her time. I told her that her story would fit perfectly in my article.

I walked to the door and looked back before exiting the diner. The boys were arguing about who would get their cone first.

I felt good about the interview with Sharon because it gave me a feel for the opinion of someone who wasn't born in Coulton and whose family didn't migrate here from overseas.

When I got home, I went straight to my bedroom and started thinking about my next interview. I hadn't yet interviewed a coal mine supervisor and thought that perspective would shed a lot of light on the company's purpose and point of view. Because the company had had such a significant impact on every aspect of people's lives in Coulton for more than a hundred years, it made sense to get their thoughts, so I planned to visit the next day.

Mom and I ate supper, and I told her all about my interview with Sharon and her twins. Mom laughed when I told her about the boys in the ice cream shop. "Boys will be boys," she said.

After breakfast, I walked to the mine office and approached the receptionist. I introduced myself, told her my reason for being there, and asked if I could make an appointment to talk with the superintendent. As she was checking his schedule, Mr. Ryan walked out of his office.

"Good morning," he said.

"Same to you," I replied.

The receptionist told him who I was and why I was there. She followed that up by saying, "Your ten o'clock appointment canceled and you have two free hours until your next appointment."

"I guess that should be just enough time for Ms. Healy to interview me," he said.

I was elated.

"Come on in and we'll get started."

We sat down, and he asked where I would like him to begin.

"I know that the mine company has a long history in Coulton," I said, "because my family has worked in the mine for three generations. Can you tell me what you know about that history?" I asked.

I've been working for the company for forty years—first as a foreman, then as the general manager, and now as superintendent. I've seen it all—deaths, injuries, cave-ins, protests, strikes, and union busting. Of course, the death of workers is always the most tragic, and having to break the sad news to families is difficult. In the years I've been here, more than fifty miners have died due to cave-ins, fires, and chemical spills. The worst happened in 1992 when a shaft in the mine was accidentally blown up by a dynamite explosion. We lost twenty miners and two office staff that day.

I still had a vivid picture in my mind of ambulances and fire trucks and rescue personnel working as hard as they could to save lives. I remembered family members running toward the mine, looking for loved ones. You could see the fear in their eyes and hear their screams as they looked for information. It was the worst day of my life.

Another issue that has disturbed me over the years was the safety concerns the miners had and the neglect of the owners. I went to bat for the miners repeatedly, and still their concerns weren't addressed. I was called in and put on the hot seat many times when I voiced my views. The answer was always the same—we've done enough. I was told that the miners need to be more careful.

Usually, the lack of effort and concern on the owners' part was because of money. As you know, there were good times and tough times for the miners. When production increased, the miners worked more and made more money, but that wasn't true when there was a huge supply of coal or the demand decreased. Then, miners were laid off or lost their jobs, which caused financial hardship for families. Strikes occurred from time to time, usually over safety, salary, and benefits. The miners' effort to create a union was the result. During those times, fights between miners and scabs broke out. Injury and sometimes death were the result. To end the strikes and continue production, the owners would throw the miners crumbs that would last until the next protest or strike.

I've read a lot about the difficulties of the miners and have concluded that both sides had fair arguments. But the greed, control, and politics that have contributed to the never-ending poverty existing in the Coulton community are things that continue to upset me.

I apologize for being so candid about my opinions, but that's the way I see it. The mine company has tried to do its best by the miners and has contributed to a number of the town's successes. Probably the most positive outcome has been the bond the community has developed over the years. Because most of the townspeople work in the mine, they've become friends for life. They depend on each other, care for those who are in need, and celebrate common interests like holidays, weddings, funerals, and other family events.

My time with the mine will end this year when I retire. It's been a good forty years, despite the fact that many families have struggled during the tough times. In a small way, I hope that my efforts to bridge the differences between the owners and miners will be judged positively.

Mr. Ryan stopped and looked at his watch. "Time's up! My next appointment is here."

I thanked him for the interview and told him that the information he shared with me would contribute significantly to my story.

On my way home, I thought about all that Mr. Ryan had told me. I was certain he would be remembered as "one of the good ones."

For my next interview, I chose Mayor Bradley because I wanted to talk to someone who was concerned about Coulton's future. I called the mayor's office and scheduled an interview for the next day at four.

When I arrived at Mayor Bradley's office in the courthouse the following day, his receptionist escorted me to his office. I explained my purpose and why I had chosen him.

"It would be my pleasure to contribute to your article and show off Coulton. Would you like to conduct the interview as we walk around town?" he asked.

"That would do nicely," I said.

Let's begin with a tour of the courthouse. Over the past hundred years plus, a variety of cases were tried in the courtroom, from murder to pickpocketing. The courthouse was built in 1908 and stood sturdy during the

1993 tornado. A few windows were broken, and some doors were blown off the hinges, but the walls and roof remained in place. My office was moved here after the tornado. The common council and the planning board meet here every month to discuss Coulton's future. Their vision is comprehensive and aggressive. During our tour, I'll point out our accomplishments thus far and talk about our future plans.

Did you know that the courthouse is thought to be haunted? As the story goes, a man was on trial for murder back in the fifties and hung himself in his cell. His cell number was twelve. After his suicide, prisoners were routinely assigned to his cell until they started complaining about a nightly visitor. Prison guards checked the cell for the hour and placed cameras, but no one ever showed. The prisoners complained that they heard a deathly scream in the night. Word got out, and whenever a new prisoner arrived, they'd want any cell but twelve. Of course, I never believed any of it—but I was never locked up in cell twelve.

Let's head outside. See that large building across the street? It was built the same year as the courthouse. It was originally a hotel and had a number of uses over the years. It's currently an indoor mall with six shops. A florist anchors one end and a gift shop the other. It was the first building renovation in Coulton in the past two years. We have other projects in the planning stages and are waiting for state and federal money.

The council has spent a lot of time reviewing Coulton's history and all the efforts that have been made to reduce poverty and make our town prosperous. Programs like the War on Poverty and VISTA and many others were tried for years but never met their goals and objectives. The attempts at improvement and betterment were always from the top down. Presidents, Congress, and governors thought that the only way for improvement was through their support. Not much thought was given to the old bootstrap approach from the bottom up. We put the responsibility in the hands of the people. That's what our council has done, and a lot of progress has been the result. We still need financial assistance from the government, but we don't need to be told what to do or how to do it. The infrastructure plan that President Biden implemented has helped a lot. New roads, mountain revitalization, water purification, broadband internet, and other economic development projects have been funded and have been a boon to our growth. The Affordable Care Act has provided health insurance to hundreds who never had it. The generational belief that mountain people are lazy and live off the government is waning. We are a proud lot, and we aim to prove it to outsiders.

See over there? That's the construction of a plaza. It'll have a grocery store, a gas and electric charging station, and a dollar store. The project will be finished this spring. And that's just the beginning. There are plans for a new hotel and other retail shops.

The old adage, if we build it, they will come, is part of the plan. We thought about how we could get visitors to come here and have relied on the state tourism department to help us. Our first endeavor was to change the perception that mountain people are uneducated and backward. We decided to change our image by having outsiders come in instead of keeping them out. We realized it would interfere with our isolated lifestyle, but to build Coulton, we had to give up something. The tough part was convincing the townspeople. Since the mine closed two years ago, many of the original families have left, but those that stayed recognized that Coulton would soon become nonexistent if something drastic wasn't done. We noticed new families leaving big cities and moving here for a more minimalistic lifestyle. When we gained their support, we were on our way.

How about we get a cup of coffee in the newly remodeled coffeehouse?

Our biggest concern was what we could do to attract visitors. Working with state tourism, we developed a plan that was bold and futuristic. We began with building on what we now have. An arts and crafts and music center will be built to market the work that has been done for years. We thought the attraction would show off our native culture. We decided to build a path alongside the creek for walking, bicycling, and jogging. We'll beautify the run-down town park and build an amphitheater. We'll host festivals throughout the year where we'll sell arts and crafts, music, and country food. The old mine barn will be rebuilt and continue to be used for family celebrations and tourist events.

When the mine shut down, we bought it and the surrounding land by paying off back taxes. We plan to board up most of it except for the entry and one shaft filled with mine memorabilia. Because the mine is the main reason Coulton exists, we want tourists to see it and learn about its history.

We had one problem—how to get the tourists to the mine. To solve this, we decided to fix the mile-long train rails, buy a passenger car, and transport tourists to and from the mine. We plan to set up a replica moonshine still in the hollow to show how moonshine is made. Also, the story about a mountain monster that has been told since the beginning of time will be a highlighted attraction to lure tourists. We are going to use the mine as the backdrop for the monster's home.

Mr. Bradley took a breath. "What do you think of our plans?" he asked.

"I'm still trying to comprehend everything you told me. It's overwhelming. If you do even half of what you described, it would be quite an accomplishment," I said. "What's the timetable for all the projects?"

"They'll be done gradually as money comes in from property taxes, state and federal government, and the hemp revenue," he said. "I forgot to mention that Jimmy Jensen's son, Joey, is writing a book titled *The History of Coulton* that will trace our town's origin and development to the present. The article you're writing will add to his project and offer a starting point for him," he said.

"I think that the term *renaissance* is applicable to your visionary plan. I look forward to seeing the changes and growth in the town I will always call home."

I thanked Mr. Badley for the tour and the coffee and for talking to me about the plans for Coulton's future. I recalled Great-Granny's and Granny's stories and thought about how proud they would be now. I was certain that the plan for Coulton was something that could be replicated throughout Appalachia and in other towns and cities in America. It could be a model for future state and federal government plans and programs to decrease poverty—but most importantly, from the bottom up and not the top down.

It was dark when I got home, and Mom had already eaten supper. She left a plate of food in the oven for me that I devoured while thinking about my latest interview.

It was January 10, and I planned to return to Lexington on the fifteenth. That gave me four more days to write my story about why I had chosen to author an article about poverty.

CHAPTER 14
OTHER TOWNS

After my last interview, I thought about other Appalachian towns that might have a similar story to tell. The Appalachian region includes thirteen states, 206,000 square miles, and hundreds of small towns. I realized it would be virtually impossible to drive to towns outside of Kentucky in a day to interview county historians. The best I could do was identify a couple of towns located close to Coulton. I located three small coal mining towns that were within a one-hundred-mile radius of Coulton. I didn't have much time before submitting my article to Ben. So, I got up early and drove to the first town located in Hazard County. I arrived at the historian's office at nine o'clock. I hoped I didn't need to make an appointment. I approached the front desk and asked if the historian was in.

"Yes, that's me. Can I help you?"

I explained my project and asked if she had time for an interview.

"I have an hour before my first meeting and would love to share what I know about Spring Valley."

"I have five questions that I would like to ask if that's okay," I said.

"That would be fine."

"Do you know who the first settlers were?"

"I believe the first immigrants to settle in Spring Valley came from the British Isles in the early 1800s. They were from Ireland and were looking for work. Coal mines were just beginning to need workers, and the Irish were welcomed. They brought a lot of their customs with them and supposedly blended in with the farming community. The new arrivals learned that they would have to adapt to a new culture, and they did very quickly. They accepted the strong adherence to God, work ethic, values, and a belief in living in isolation."

"Did they participate in local customs like music, dance, and art?"

"Yes, they did. As a matter of fact, they became more involved in local customs than the original settlers."

"Do you know if their assimilation created a bond among poor whites, Black people, and rich whites?"

"Yes, that bond has stayed with the community since their arrival."

"I noticed that Spring Valley has fallen on hard times since the mine closed. What has been done to revive the once-active town?"

"Not much has been done because there's no money or desire among the remaining residents to search for alternatives. I'm afraid Spring Valley is on its last leg and is destined to become a ghost town."

"Where have all the people gone?"

"Most have left for the big northern cities for work and a better life. Those remaining are old and their futures are bleak."

An hour had passed, and Mrs. Brown was anxious to get to her meeting. I thanked her for the information and headed to Sulfur Ridge. It took me an hour to get there. I found the historical building next to the courthouse. At first glance, Sulfur Ridge looked to be quite prosperous. The town was quaint. Small antique shops, retail stores, and a couple of restaurants lined the sidewalks. I walked into the historical society building and asked the receptionist if the historian was available.

"No, she's out for the day and won't be back till early morning," she said.

An elderly lady heard me and asked if she could help. She was very energetic and reminded me of Granny.

"Well, I wanted to talk to the historian about the town's history."

"I can help you with that. I've been here for eighty-seven years. What do you want to know?"

I explained my reason for being there. I decided to change my question-and-answer approach and asked her to tell me as much as she knew.

"My family came to Sulfur Ridge in the late 1920s," she said. "We migrated from Scotland and decided this was a good place to live and work. The coal mine was booming, and work was easy to get. Our family and others blended in with the existing population and were accepted by most. We struggled at times just like most of the families, but we kept our noses to the grindstone and never let the town go down. We are a churchgoing bunch that has worked hard our whole lives. When times were tough, we supported one another and always survived. When the mining company shut down, we decided to create a welcoming environment for tourists. As you might have seen, we have restored our old buildings and created a bunch of shops. We get a lot of visitors on the weekends who enjoy what we have to offer. Most of the residents are new and have relocated here from large cities for a more laid-back lifestyle. They brought their businesses and skills with them, and today we are a successful mountain town looking to the future."

I was thrilled with the information Mrs. George shared and felt it would complement my article.

I felt comfortable with all the interviews and believed the personalized stories, both first and secondhand, would offer a realistic picture for my readers.

CHAPTER 15
MY STORY

I was approaching the end, and I asked myself two questions. Why am I writing about the poor? Are my experiences credible enough?

I thought about my early childhood and my growth to adulthood as I searched for answers to my questions. I realized that there was a period in my life where I felt my poorness very deeply. The feeling began after my father died when I was eleven years old. I truly can't remember much of my life before then. I grew up in a middle-class family on a street with seventy-five families. I knew the exact number because I delivered the evening newspaper to their doors for five years. We were the only family on the street who lost their father. My mother was a full-time office worker and was gone five days a week, nine hours a day. I had three siblings. One was older, and two were younger. After my father died, I assumed the role of protector, not even questioning whether a skinny, hundred pound, 4'11", eleven-year-old could defend the family if needed.

I didn't live in poverty, and I couldn't even say I was poor. But I knew that we didn't have the money that other families did, and I was limited in the material things I could have. My mother made enough money to pay the monthly mortgage, keep up with the utility bills, and buy food. There was never a night I didn't have a balanced meal, and I never went to bed hungry. My mother made fudge or popcorn on Saturday bath nights. Those were my special treats. I realized early on there was no money for extras. My mother bought me new sneakers at the beginning of each school year, and they had to last through the summer. If the sneaker sole broke away, I glued it until I got a new pair. When I had holes in the heels of my socks, I would pull the sock down under the heel so it wouldn't be seen. During the winter, if the metal buckles on my black rubber boots broke off, I used a rubber band or tape to close the front.

At Christmas, clothes, food, and a tree were donated to needy families by Catholic Charities or The Holy Name Society. Yes, I was raised a Catholic and even had thoughts of becoming a priest until I reached eighth grade and Jane Hadley came to school with a tightly knit sweater. That changed my mind. It was the first time I realized that our anatomies were different.

For young adolescents, clothes were important. After my mother paid for living expenses, there wasn't much left, so I wore the same outfits routinely—but there was never a concern about my clothes being clean. My mother washed our clothes every Saturday and made sure they were ready Monday morning.

Church, for me, was important. It had a lot to do with developing my strong values, ethics, and morals. I remember one time when I had to serve 6:30 a.m. mass on Christmas morning. I had gotten a new pair of Wrangler dungarees and wore them to church. I was putting on my cassock when one of the older altar boys, who was dressed in a white shirt and tie, commented on my chosen outfit. I quit being an altar boy that week! That incident influenced my feelings about being poor more than any other. I never asked for more than my mother could provide from that day forward.

Not having a father also added to my feelings about being poor. All the guys on the street had fathers, and they spent time with each other. I would observe fathers playing catch in their driveways, kids being driven to ballgames, or fathers and sons just sitting together on their front porches. Those were the times I felt really poor. To compensate for not having a father, I identified role models and observed their interactions with their sons. I envied their relationships.

When I got to high school, I became a good athlete. I played three sports and loved the attention I got from my schoolmates. I lost some of my feelings about being poor but struggled with loneliness and the desire to improve my academics. I wasn't an "*A*" student, but I always wished I were. My social life was limited because I didn't have the money to date or buy better clothes. I had plenty of friends and enjoyed playing sports and hanging out with them.

During my senior year, I recognized that there were three options for me when I graduated—steel plant, army, or college. I had worked in a pancake house as a dishwasher, busboy, and cook for a couple of years and had saved five hundred dollars. I heard about a small college in Kentucky that cost exactly that amount for one semester. I applied, got accepted, and took a Greyhound bus to college. I had bought two "leather" suitcases at a pawn shop for the journey. After three bus changes, I retrieved my tattered and torn suitcases.

One of my good friends, Steve, went with me. It was the first time I had left Buffalo, NY, and I didn't know what to expect. When Steve and I arrived, we walked from the station to the dorm, but on the way, I stopped in a men's room. Above the urinal, there was a sign that said, "We hate WOPS. Yankees go home." That was my welcome to the post-Civil War Kentucky town. I walked to the newly built air-conditioned dorm. I'd never had the luxury of AC and enjoyed every minute of it because of the ninety-seven-degree weather. My seven-day meal ticket didn't begin till registration, which was two days away, so I filled up on chips and candy until I got my ticket.

On the second day in my new home, I decided to venture out of the dorm for breakfast. I walked off campus and stumbled on a diner. There was a sign above the door—*College Diner – Welcome Back Students*. It looked friendly enough, so I went in and sat at the counter.

A waitress dressed in street clothes approached. "What'll you have, hon?" she asked.

"Orange juice, bacon, toast, and two eggs," I replied.

"How do you want your eggs? Do you want biscuits, gravy, and grits with that?"

"Over-easy, and toast will be fine," I said. I wasn't familiar with biscuits and gravy for breakfast, and I had never heard of grits.

While I waited for my meal, I checked out the restaurant's interior. Above the cook's window was a Confederate flag, and below the flag was a double-barrel shotgun. I glanced to the right of the main counter and saw a door with a sign above it that said, "Whites Only." On the opposite side of the counter, a sign above the door said, "Coloreds Only." My exposure to discrimination and racism was nonexistent. I had gone to all-white schools, and the only diversity I experienced was a couple of foreign exchange students.

The waitress arrived and put my order on the counter. She didn't say anything, wasn't friendly, and walked away abruptly. So much for Southern hospitality. I gobbled my food, paid the bill, and left. As the door slammed shut, I heard the waitress yell, "Y'all come back now, you hear."

As I walked back to the dorm, I thought about my upbringing in the North. Had I been so sheltered that I didn't know that there was a distinct difference in the attitude of some Southerners toward Northerners? The Civil Rights Act couldn't come too soon.

The cafeteria doors opened the next day, and my seven-day meal plan allowed three meals a day in a new air-conditioned cafeteria. I thought I had died and gone to heaven.

Because I didn't have extra money, I worked as a janitor for the college. I didn't socialize much other than with guys from Jersey and NYC.

ROTC was mandatory for the first two years, so every week, I had to put on my uniform and assemble in the campus communal area. There were strict requirements for untarnished brass buckles, unshined black-toe shoes, three military creases on the back of your shirt, a clean-shaven face, and no long hair. I bought Brasso for my buckle, plastic spray for my shoes, and used the dorm iron for my creases. I bought a supply of razors and found a barber to cut my hair. The expenses for ROTC totaled ten dollars a month—money I didn't have. During the second semester of my sophomore year, I was placed in the "Goon Platoon" and couldn't participate in any of the weekly assemblies and marches. I was happy! The Vietnam War had begun, and US involvement was only a matter of time. During my senior year, I had begun to take a position on the war—I didn't like it.

There were a number of fraternities on campus that were divided between Southerners and Northerners. I remained independent and concentrated on my studies and graduating in four years. The years flew by quickly. I learned how to study and graduated with majors in English and history and a minor in education.

I met my Kentucky wife at the end of my senior year, got married, and returned to a suburban school district in Buffalo, where I taught seventh-grade English for three years. After I got married and had a steady income, my feelings about being poor dissipated. I had a minor setback when my wife and three-month-old daughter went to graduate school. We ran out of money during the second semester and went on food stamps.

When I finished graduate school, I became a teacher for the deaf, a speech and language therapist, an educational center principal, and a consultant. As a therapist, I made a number of home visits in rural communities. I observed the daily lives of the poorest of the poor. In my role as a principal, I tracked the free breakfast and lunch numbers. Ninety percent of the families received assistance. I made an occasional home visit and witnessed horrible living conditions—falling-down houses, leaky roofs, turned-off utilities, tattered and torn clothing, and a lack of nutritional food.

As a state consultant, I traveled to all the Kentucky regions, but I spent a lot of time in Eastern Kentucky (Appalachia). I observed the living conditions of poor white and Black families. Barefoot, dirty, and hungry children. Parents trying to make ends meet with no positive results in sight. During my mountain travels, I drove through abandoned towns with no one in sight. There were boarded-up buildings, fallen trees, and vacant schools. Posted signs on telephone poles warned, "Polluted water! Don't drink." I observed the results of strip and mountaintop mining. Mountainsides were flattened and void of trees, rockslides left roads impassable, and poisoned water streamed into creeks.

When I began writing this book, I questioned whether I understood the definition and characteristics of being poor and had the credibility to write about poverty. However, my personal and professional life experiences offer credibility that I know it well.

CONCLUSION

It was January 14, and I finished the first edit of my book. I planned to leave for Lexington the next day. Mom was quiet the night before I left, and I sensed she had become used to me being around for a month. I asked her to come to Lexington to live with me, but she said she was born in Coulton and planned to die in Coulton. I went to bed that night thinking about all the interviews, whether my story would be read, and if it was good enough to improve the newspaper's circulation. Ben had the promos printed in anticipation of my article. Bobbie Joe had called a couple of times to inform me that he hadn't found an apartment yet. I guessed I'd have a roommate when I got home.

I got up early the next morning. I had already packed my suitcase and was ready for the journey. Mom hugged me goodbye, and I hopped in my car for the hour-long drive to Lexington. I decided that my first stop would be my newspaper office.

When I got into the building, I met Ben in the lobby. "Are you ready to make the final changes to your article?" he asked.

"I'm close, but I want to do another edit before I give it to you," I replied.

We walked up the stairs to the reporters' room. Ben went to his office, and I went to my desk. I was nervous about the article being approved by him and whether anyone would want to read it. It took me two days to edit because I was afraid it wouldn't be received well. At the end of the second day, I forwarded the article to Ben and hoped for the best.

The next day, he walked into my office and told me the article would be published in the next Saturday Review section of the paper.

"How do you think it'll be received?" I asked.

"You never know. Some will like it, and some won't, but that's not the most important thing. You put your heart and soul into it, and that's what matters. It may or may not improve circulation, but we gave it our best shot," he said. He walked toward the door, turned, and winked at me. His last comment was, "That's journalism for you."

I got up from my chair and put my coat on, wondering what was happening at my apartment. When I got there, I opened the door to find Bobbie Joe standing in front of the stove.

"Thought you might be hungry, so I'm making a stir fry," he said.

"Sounds good to me," I replied.

The night went by quickly. Bobbie Joe and I got along well, and I enjoyed his company.

I went to work the rest of the week, knowing that the first segment of my article would hit the newsstands, homes, and the internet on Saturday. I was nervous and could hardly wait for Monday morning. I got to my office early and opened my email messages. There were fifty-one responses. I opened the first message. It was from a woman who had grown up in an Appalachian coal town. She said that my article brought back memories and she looked forward to the next segment. The next three messages were also positive. The fourth was not. It said my information was inaccurate and I should do more research. I was given a plan to follow. I read the remaining messages. Thirty-two were positive, six were maybes, and the remainder were negative. I concentrated on the negative responses to determine why my readers had problems with the article. Some indicated they had little knowledge of Appalachia, and the rest I identified as outsiders who had been listening to false stories for years. I made the decision to stick with the article the way I had written it and let the cards fall where they may.

Over the next four weeks that the article was published, I received over five hundred responses. Most of them were positive, which encouraged me. Because the percentage of positive responses was good, I thought the article might help the paper reach the subscription goal.

I walked to Ben's office and told him about the messages.

"As I said before, you win some, and you lose some. Keep me posted," he said.

The week was long, but the trend held. The article was published four more weekends with the same results—more positives than negatives. But the important question was still left unanswered. Had circulation improved? Ben had been monitoring this and advised me that there was a 10 percent increase in home and online sales. Although we were both satisfied with that result, the increase was certainly not enough to suggest that the newspaper was on solid ground. Ben recommended a follow-up with more articles about social issues. I took his advice and began writing about women's reproductive rights, mass murders, school shootings, gun laws, and a host of other issues I thought were both controversial and important. I was careful to stay neutral and be as objective as possible to create an avenue of dialogue and open communication.

After two months, I realized that I wanted to discuss issues directly with an audience, so I created a podcast that was broadcast weekly via an open mic. There was no screening, and anyone could participate with one caveat—if a participant violated a set of rules, communication was canceled immediately. The rules were disclosed and agreed to before an airing. I enjoyed the podcast approach more than writing articles and decided to place an emphasis on them. I created an outline of topics and posted them with weekly dates. The first topic was poverty. I posted three questions to be answered by my audience. How would you define poverty? Can you give concrete examples of real poverty? How can poverty be decreased? The responses I received varied, but for the most part, my audience gave good answers to all three questions. More important to me was their encouragement to post even more topics. I was thrilled with the response, and the number of followers steadily increased.

By the end of the first week, I had thousands of internet and podcast followers. I thought the percentage of positive responses was good and was encouraged. Ben had been reading my article and following my podcast. He was equally excited about my success and the increase in the newspaper's circulation.

I continued to receive messages during the week about my articles and podcasts. Some were more positive than others. I could hardly wait to see the messages after each segment. The week was long, but the trend held. There were more positives. The article was published three more weekends with the same results. I thought it was successful, but the most important question still hung in the air. How much would circulation improve? At the end of the last article segment, Ben advised me that there had been a 15 percent increase in home and online sales. The owners were pleased, and we were happy.

The *Gazette* recognized my work, as did other newspapers. I was approached more than once during the year but didn't accept an offer. I liked my work, and the approval rating was high, but on a personal level, I had to decide whether I wanted to leave Lexington. The major item that was holding me back was my roommate.

I left the office late Friday evening and drove to my apartment. Bobbie Joe had planned for us to go out for dinner, but I decided I wanted to do something important. I opened the door, and he greeted me with a kiss.

"Do you still want to go out for dinner?" he asked.

"Let's stay in and cook something," I said.

After we'd finished dinner and cleaned up, we sat on the couch with a glass of wine. I wasn't sure how I wanted to start the conversation, so I asked, "How's school going?"

"My year ended well, but it's a slow process," he said.

"I know what you mean. To complete the requirements in the next three years will be tough."

"I know, but I'll do it," he said. "How are things at the paper?"

"Going well, and that's something I want to talk to you about. I've been approached by a couple of newspapers about working for them, but it would require me to relocate. I'm still mulling over the offers."

"If you think the timing is good, I say go for it," he said.

"But I'm worried how it will affect your plans."

"Don't worry about me. I always land with my feet firmly on the ground," he said.

I sat back and thought. I didn't think Bobbie Joe got the message, so I tried again. "How would a move affect our relationship?" I asked.

He didn't say anything for a couple of minutes and then looked at me. "We're getting along well, and I'm ready to take our relationship to the next level if you are."

He got the message. "You know, we haven't talked about a future together till now. I'm ready to make a commitment. How about we see how things go with my job and with us for another year and go from there," I said.

"You mean we're officially boyfriend and girlfriend now?" he asked.

We laughed, hugged, and kissed.

"Let's go out to eat and celebrate our new relationship," he said. I agreed.

EPILOGUE

I CONTINUED TO WORK AT THE *GAZETTE* for a year, and Bobbie Joe completed more of the requirements for his mechanical engineering degree. We were getting along great and sharing the same bedroom.

Mom was firmly planted in Coulton and incredibly happy. I visited during the holidays to catch up with Sally Mae, Willie, and Paul. But more importantly, I wanted to check on the town's progress.

Bobbie Joe and I drove down for Thanksgiving. As we approached the top of the mountain that overlooked the valley, I saw the same housing separation that had existed since Great-Granny first arrived in Coulton, but there seemed to be a number of new buildings, and one that stuck out from the others. That four-story building was the Coulton Hotel and Inn. I was impressed and planned to take a tour around town to see the other changes.

I had a fear that the changes would affect the people. After we settled in at Mom's house, I decided to go to the tavern. Sally Mae had already made her appearance, and we greeted each other with hugs. We caught up on her work, my work, and Bobbie Joe. I saw a couple of high school friends and chatted with them.

"How do you like the changes to our town," one of them asked.

"I haven't seen much yet. What's your opinion?"

"We like everything. There are more jobs, and people are making more money. We get a lot of tourists coming through, and the response has been very positive. Even some of the old-timers like how things are now. It sure is different from the old days when the only game in town was mining. The townspeople are working as hard as ever, and they're seeing satisfactory results. The image of us being hillbillies has changed because the outsiders are going back home telling people about the positives."

It was like we had become a whole new entity with a bright future. One thing that made most of the townspeople happy was that our town was built by 'insiders.' The cultural bond that had evolved for hundreds of years still existed and was preserved for future generations.

AFTERWORD

I CHOSE TO WRITE ABOUT POVERTY in a small Eastern Kentucky coal town because I wanted to describe the cultural norms that have been handed down from generation to generation.

As I wrote, I felt that I needed to dispel the negative rumors and stories that have been told and written about Appalachia. I decided to concentrate on the town's cultural growth over time and the bond that its residents developed. It struck me early in my writing that the only way a culture could be preserved was to turn a negative into a positive. With that in mind, I built a story where the residents took control of their own destiny. They adhered to their beliefs and customs through adversities. They never wavered, and success was eventually achieved.

Although the story is fictional, I believe there are many Appalachian coal towns with similar stories. The resiliency that the residents possess has been challenged for hundreds of years. Despite a multitude of hardships, coal-town people have survived to overcome poverty. I believe they will continue to do so no matter who or what gets in their way.

www.ingramcontent.com/pod-product-compliance
Lightning Source LLC
LaVergne TN
LVHW010316070526
838199LV00065B/5581